I0564984

ELUSIVE BEINGS

A SHADE OF MIND
BOOK THREE

OUTLANDERS OF THE MULTIVERSE
COLLECTION

BY D.N. LEO

Narrative Land Publishing
Narrativeland.com

A Shade of Mind
http://narrativeland.com/shade

1-4 Random Psychic
2-4 Forever Mortal
3-4 Elusive Beings
4-4 Imperfect Divine

Elusive Beings

Synopsis

Ciaran survives the fight for the truth behind the crucifix, but it has triggered an even bigger disaster that might tear Ciaran and Madeline apart forever. The truth behind the crucifix is trivial compared to the catastrophes built into the aftermath. To solve these crises, Ciaran and Madeline face a basic but difficult question—who are they, really?

This third installment in an urban fantasy thriller series, filled with romance and science fiction twists and turns, will take you to the deepest corners of the minds of those who dare to sacrifice.

CHAPTER 1

The stench of fresh blood engulfed Madeline. She stormed into the living room of a country house in the middle of the Australian outback. With one hand still clinging to a fish basket and the other gripping a fishing spear, she approached the entrance of the adjacent reception room with caution.

She wanted to call out for Jo but thought that would be unwise.

It had been Jo's idea to travel all the way from New York for an exotic celebration of Jo's eighteenth birthday. Madeline hoped it didn't turn into the last trip of her life.

Madeline went out for the afternoon to take lessons from an Australian Aboriginal on how to catch fish the ancient way. They were going to have a surprise dinner for Jo tonight—a surprise because Jo disliked fish and Madeline didn't cook.

Luckily for them, the dinner was Zach's idea. He was their mutual Australian friend. Zach would turn twenty-one soon and planned to put the cozy kitchen of the small guest house to good use to celebrate a double birthday.

Blood.

It was all she could see in the reception room— amid the broken furniture.

Hesitating no more, Madeline yelled, "Jo!"

A cacophony of sounds—crashing glass, pots, pans, and other kitchen objects and a bloodcurdling scream—came in response, sending Madeline racing toward the kitchen.

More blood.

That was what she found. At the corner of the kitchen, Jo was on the floor, unconscious. Zach stood next to her, guarding her immobile body.

Zach's shirt was soaked in blood. He didn't look like he would be able to stand for long.

Larry, the host of the guest house, brandished a knife with one hand and held the other hand to his ear, screaming as if his head was going to explode. He reeled back and forth, crashing into the kitchen furniture and knocking it over.

There was no sign of his wife and children, but Madeline saw blood trailing out of the kitchen and through the door leading to the family room.

Larry was in his late sixties, a soft-spoken man and kind father and husband who had housed them for three days. That had been Larry before she'd finished her fishing lesson. But it wasn't the Larry before her now.

Zach was cornered. "Run, Madeline," Zach yelled.

She stood right at the door, not moving. She knew what was going on. "Is Jo alive?"

"Yes. Run, Madeline! He's insane. He's not listening, so don't even try to talk to him."

Larry directed his bloodshot eyes at Madeline. There was no humanity in him that she could see. The devil had taken over. An explicable smirk crossed his face as he approached her.

"Run, Madeline!" Zach yelled again and this time he captured Larry's attention. The old man swung his head back toward Zach.

Madeline threw the fish basket at Larry, hitting him in the head.

As soon as the basket left her hand she could smell it—the metallic stench from her ghost.

Larry turned to walk toward her, and Zach took the opportunity to charge him from behind. Larry suddenly swung back, and the knife in his hand slashed at Zach's abdomen. He grabbed Zach's neck with one hand and waved the knife with the other.

He was going to slaughter Zach.

Madeline knew Larry's strength was not his own. It was not his soul inside his body. "Larry, stop!" Madeline said firmly.

He released Zach instantly, dropping him to the floor unconscious to lie next to Jo. Then he turned to Madeline. Smirking, he walked toward her like a zombie. He didn't even threaten her with the knife to give her an excuse to kill him in self-defense. He simply staggered toward her with a crazed smile on his face.

In his eyes, she could still see the pledge of the kind old man who had been their friend for the last three days. She knew he was innocent.

He must have been the one who killed his wife and kids. But his body was only doing what it was being told to do.

The metallic stench of her ghost grew stronger. It was not the first time the ghost had possessed men to kill. All she had to do to end all this was to kill the man in front of her.

Once and for all, it would end.

But the old man was innocent.

She had never been able to do that, to end it, and the ghost kept coming back. Disaster after disaster. And people would continue to be murdered until she killed the host the ghost possessed.

Larry continued to approach Madeline.

"Don't come any closer." She stepped back.

Larry kept coming. She could see his eyes had started to clear. Once that happened, he would return to normal and see what he'd just done. Most often, the men, after being possessed, went insane and eventually killed themselves.

"Your last chance, Madeline. Keep your virtuous soul, and more people will die," an ancient voice echoed in the air.

She had to kill this innocent man for the craziness to end. The ghost had been telling her that for years—it would continue to kill until she killed an innocent man. But no matter how she tried to justify it, in front of her was a helpless man whom she had no right to kill.

Larry took another step toward her.

"Time is running out, Madeline. Next time, it will be worse," the ghost chanted.

"Stop, Larry!"

She yelled at the old man, but he kept advancing. She raised the fishing spear, pointing it at his heart.

CHAPTER 2

*T*en years later.

It was after six in the morning, but Madeline couldn't find any sign of the winter sun. She overanalyzed the humidity, the feel of the air, and the sound of the wind, concluding that England winters and New York winters were the same—cold and bleak.

Ciaran turned away from the window and looked at her.

Madeline should have gotten used to the sight of Ciaran by now, but it never happened. God must have been in a very good mood indeed when he created such a gorgeous human being. She could hardly believe that every inch of that six foot three slender yet muscular warrior's body belonged to her. His face—that of a dark angel—continued to make her stomach quiver. Those deep and intense gray eyes focused on her as if for him no one else existed and nothing else in the world mattered.

Suddenly a bullet hit Ciaran's chest, exiting from his back. Blood splattered onto the glass window. Madeline gasped as the image of Ciaran flickered and disappeared.

She shook her head and snapped back to reality. A few days ago, her life had changed forever.

She still remembered the sensation of Ciaran's blood on her hands, the commotion in the operation room, and the emptiness when she thought her world would exist without him in it.

She couldn't get the memory of his beautiful eyes, glassed over and lifeless, out of her mind. And she couldn't ignore the lingering fear that she would have to experience that incident again in the future. Ciaran said he had left the memory behind to move on with life, to be with her. But that was before she told him the truth behind his recovery.

It wasn't a miracle that he was back with her again.

Jennifer had wanted her to tell Ciaran, and she had. But regardless of how much she tried to spin the story and make it golden, the naked truth was that his mother had swapped the drug. And, as a result, Juliette had died, and the real drug had coincidentally saved his life.

Jennifer had told her that Juliette never let go of anything, and Madeline wagered she would cling to Ciaran this time more than at any other time.

This ordeal wasn't over yet. Not by a long shot.

The air seemed to thicken a bit. Madeline spun around, surveying the empty room around her. She didn't care for what she was feeling. This wasn't her familiar psychic blue dots. It wasn't the appearance of Juliette's hologram, either.

It was the unmistakable metallic stench of her long forgotten ghost. *Who was it going to possess now?* Fear rose in her mind like tidal waves.

"Madeline!"

Madeline startled and cried out.

"Are you okay?" Tadgh said from the door. "I knocked." Tadgh stood, puzzled, his hands in his pockets.

"Huh?"

"Can I have a word with you?"

"Of course." Madeline smiled. "Where's Jo?"

"Planning a new game in the game room . . ."

Madeline was a bit disturbed by Tadgh's apparent agitation as he rolled up and down on the balls of his feet. "What's up Tadgh?" she asked.

"I don't know. Something feels strange."

"Why wouldn't it seem that way, especially after all that's happened?"

"I called Dublin. They said Mother hasn't arrived home yet. She left ages ago. Where could she be?"

"Is there anywhere she might go to take some time off? Be by herself? She's been through a lot lately. What about your cousin George's in France? Jennifer mentioned him before."

Tadgh shook his head. "You don't know my mother. She's an authoritative figure in the family. She would never take shelter anywhere or protection from anyone—no matter how mad Ciaran might be at her. I even searched for air traffic info just in case . . ."

"There might have been an accident?"

Tadgh nodded. "Air, road, water . . . I looked everywhere. I even rang George, although I knew it was entirely unlikely that she'd gone to France. I couldn't find a hint of her. What did she say to you?"

"Nothing. She just cried."

"Do you . . ." Tadgh cleared his throat, "Do you think Mother did the right thing, you know, regarding Juliette?"

"I won't judge her, Tadgh. One day, I will be a mother, too, and I don't know what I would do or what I will be capable of when it comes to the welfare of my own children."

Tadgh nodded.

"Let me see what I can do," Madeline said and closed her eyes. She tried to catch a sense of Jennifer's mind—a trace, a feel, a hint of even a single blue dot somewhere.

A dot suddenly appeared at the back of her mind, quickly expanding and exploding like a bomb, spraying dark blood particles all over her. The metallic stench engulfed her senses.

Madeline yelped and slumped to the floor.

"Madeline, are you okay?" Tadgh ran to her, holding her by the shoulders and sitting her up.

"Do you smell anything strange in the room, Tadgh?"

He squinted his nose, sniffed, then shook his head. "Why? What's going on?"

She shook her head. "I can't see your mother, Tadgh."

"That's okay."

"I'll keep looking," Madeline promised.

"Where's Ciaran?" Tadgh asked.

Madeline smiled. "He said he was going out for some fresh air . . ." Her voice trailed off. She could swear that she had just seen the white Mountain Avens flowers she'd picked this morning bleeding. She'd watched as a drop of blood formed at the center of a single flower, rolled down a white petal, and landed on the table. She blinked, looking again closely.

Ciaran had said this was Juliette's favorite kind of flower, and he'd had them brought here from Ireland.

Tadgh frowned. "Are you okay, Madeline? Tell me what's going on."

"What color are those flowers over there, Tadgh?"

"They're white. Why do you ask?"

"Was Juliette by any chance buried near here?"

Tadgh cocked an eyebrow. "You want to buy her flowers?"

"Was she cremated or buried?"

"She was buried. The family's cemetery is nearby. Why?"

She wondered whether her ghost was able to possess an already dead body. Her mind's eye kept seeing the Mountain Avens dropping blood onto the table—it seems like an omen or a warning to her. She closed her eyes, concentrated, and traced Ciaran's thoughts.

Madeline muttered. "Ciaran is at the cemetery at the moment. Trouble's coming. I can feel it. He didn't bring his cell with him. We have to go there right away."

"Can't you channel to him, talk to him in your mind? You know, using your psychic trick."

"It's not a trick, Tadgh, it's an ability. And yes, I can channel and try to communicate with Ciaran. But he's not a psychic—he can't hear me and can't respond."

"Okay. Let's go then. Hope it's not too late. What's he thinking, not bringing his cell with him?"

"Nostalgia," Madeline muttered.

Tadgh led the way, and they rushed out of the room.

CHAPTER 3

The bleak morning couldn't possibly weigh down the air at the cemetery any further than it already was. Rows and rows of graves lined up neatly in the grass. Even in death, the LeBlancs protected their privacy, and their private family plots were located at the far corner of the cemetery. Ciaran squinted at the sight of Tadgh and Madeline racing toward the tomb.

It started to drizzle.

Madeline rushed into the tomb and glanced around. She looked nervous—and she should be. He had managed to drag her into the tangled mess of his past in no time. He pulled Madeline into his arms as soon as she ran inside, holding her tightly until every muscle in his body quivered with emotion. In the corner, Tadgh shook rainwater from his coat.

Suddenly, the air thickened. Ciaran knew what it was, and he didn't care for it one bit.

It meant trouble.

"Tadgh, get out of here. Now!" Ciaran called out to his brother.

As the candle in the tomb flickered, and the faint but sharp smell of burning electrical current rushed through the room, a hologram of Juliette appeared. Ciaran wasn't at all surprised to see it—someone had simulated her image, and he had seen it in the hologame.

But he was stunned at how the raw emotion flooded back to him, seeing her this close and this real again.

She wore a red dress and stood next to the altar, smiling graciously at him.

"You killed my brother, Ciaran."

"He nearly killed me, too." Ciaran moved Madeline behind him protectively, almost squashing her against the wall.

"Yes, you're right. You told me that before. But in battle, someone always gets hurt."

"What do you want, whoever you are?"

"I'm Juliette," she said. "*Your* Juliette. Or I was once. I died on Earth because of you. My father traded his life to get me out of here. And now you've killed my brother. So it's only fair to ask you to come back to me, isn't it? All you have to do is to go through the gate."

"What gate?"

"The Daimon Gate. All of the information you need is on the disk I hid at Mon Ciel. Process the disk, and then you'll be able to see the gate. Come here and be with me."

"I don't have the disk."

Juliette nodded. "Oh, it's that old man Richard again, isn't it? He got the disk, didn't he? But he won't know how to decode it. Not everyone is as smart as you and me, Ciaran. You need to find the disk and decode it." She smiled again. "I miss you."

"And what if he won't go through the gate?" Madeline asked.

Juliette laughed. "Oh, sister. Of course, you'd ask such a foolish question. You do think you have a claim on my man."

The holographic Juliette cast an evil eye at Madeline. Ciaran moved forward slightly.

"You're no competition for Madeline," Ciaran told the hologram. "You can't compare yourself with the innocent Juliette I loved years ago. You're an electronic profile. Nothing more. Juliette died. You might be able to simulate her emotions and experiences, but you can't simulate the real love we had for each other."

"I *am* your Juliette! I didn't die!" The hologram whirled back and forth. Its skin grew radiant and red.

"You just told me that you died on Earth because of me. That was a lie?"

"No. I did die on Earth. But I live elsewhere now. You have to be with me. You have to go through the gate."

Tadgh sneered. "So you're in hell now? I would say heaven, but given what you did, I wouldn't think heaven would take you."

"Tadgh!" Ciaran warned him. He didn't want to make the hologram angry. He had a feeling it wasn't just a simple hologram with familiar properties. This hologram was something more, something new and more tangible. It might be able to do some real damage.

Tadgh continued. "As far as I'm concerned, Stefan shot my brother, and he got a bullet in return. That's a tit for a tat. You see, in battle, as you said, someone always gets hurt. If you had told Ciaran your motives from the beginning, you would never have been in a relationship with him, let alone in love and married. You cheated first. Unfortunately—like brother, like sister—you paid a consequence. I can't see that my brother owes you anything. We're done here."

"Tadgh is right. I owe you nothing, Juliette. Let me have my fond memories of you—and you stay wherever you are. I can't—I won't—join you." He tried to be firm, but Ciaran knew it wasn't going to work.

He pushed Madeline toward the door. The burned smell in the air thickened and grew stronger. They heard the faint sound of crackling wires and dry wood burning. "No one walks away from me." Juliette's face turned dark red, and then purple. "Including you." Her eyes filled with rage. "I won't allow it!"

Ciaran grabbed Madeline and called out for Tadgh, "Run!"

Madeline and Ciaran charged out of the tomb.

The hologram whirled and spun. The light circle around it extended until it became a gigantic cylinder.

It grew larger by the second, turning into a small tornado. It stirred the air and sucked everything loose inside the tomb into its vortex. It spun objects around and ejected them randomly in different directions.

It lifted a tombstone and threw it to the ground, breaking it into pieces. It unearthed a coffin and spun the lid away into the air. The tornado grew and exploded the tomb. Shards of rock and concrete rained down on the cemetery grounds.

Madeline, Ciaran, and Tadgh ran. They heard the explosion behind them, but they did not look back.

The tornado built up size and speed quickly. It rose into the darkening sky.

It grew. It chased.

Ciaran looked back and could see the tornado's need to devour. It would indiscriminately suck everyone and everything into it. But he knew its quest—it wanted only him.

CHAPTER 4

The funnel of wind and suction followed right behind them. Ciaran knew Juliette wanted him. He slowed down and shoved hard at Tadgh's and Madeline's backs. As they fell forward, the tornado drew him in.

Suddenly, it stopped expanding. It withdrew at high speed, away from Tadgh and Madeline.

Ciaran could feel every bone in his body rattling as he flew around in circles inside the wind tunnel of the tornado. It spun him around, and his body crashed into the various objects whirling around with him—trees, walls, stones.

As he came around each time, he could see Madeline in the distance, trying to run at the tornado. Tadgh held her back.

She yelled, seemingly speaking to the air, "Grandfather, if you are the one who sent Juliette, please stop her! I'll go with you! I'll go wherever you want. Just release Ciaran!"

Ciaran's body dropped to the ground in the center of the funnel after hitting the top of a tree. He spat out blood as he hit the ground hard. His wound had reopened and started to bleed.

Tadgh charged the tornado, trying to get to his brother. The wind wall spun him away, tossing him against a tombstone like he was a mere pebble. There was no way Tadgh would be able to penetrate the circle of wind. It was too powerful.

Ciaran shook his head. "You can't get in, Tadgh. Don't hurt yourself." Ciaran was in the center of the whirling storm. He appeared to be in the eye of the tornado. He leaned on a tree and slowly pulled himself to his feet.

The holographic Juliette appeared next to him and smiled. "Welcome to my world. You're mine now, Ciaran. Forever. Dead or alive." She reached her hand out to grab him.

Her hand would have been cut off had she not withdrawn it quickly enough. A blue lightning bolt struck right between Ciaran and Juliette. Confused and angry, Juliette staggered a few steps backward.

In the middle of the tornado, the woman who stood between Juliette and Ciaran was as beautiful as an angel.

Ciaran stepped closer to the woman. She wore a long, white robe with a furred hood. He could not see her hair, but Ciaran guessed it was long, wavy, and as white as clouds. Her milky skin was almost transparent, and her big blue eyes were striking and oddly familiar.

Ciaran had seen those eyes before.

Unlike Juliette, this woman was not a hologram. The energy coming from her warmed the air around him. He could feel her physical presence.

"Ayana Dee," Juliette grunted with resentment.

Ayana gave Ciaran a warm glance and a gentle smile. Then, she quickly whirled around, snapping at Juliette. "You injured a successor. You are now exiled."

"Since when is he a successor?" Juliette growled.

Ayana grabbed Ciaran's left arm to reveal the golden crucifix tattoo. She pressed her thumb onto Ciaran's left arm. The contact burned his flesh, glowed, and sparked out some flames.

Ciaran grunted in pain. It felt as if his body was going to disintegrate. Every cell seemed to shift, wanting to move away from the cell next to it. He slumped to the ground.

"His successor position has now been sealed." Ayana studied the burn mark on Ciaran's arm with satisfaction. She pulled him up and spun him outside the circle of wind that had imprisoned him.

Ciaran's body rolled across the ground toward Madeline and Tadgh, and they darted toward him. Ciaran sat up and spat out more blood onto the ground. His insides felt like mashed potatoes. Everything around him appeared to be floating in a haze.

"Biological imprint. That's Bran's seal. I am authorized to activate it," Ayana said.

"But Ciaran didn't give his consent," Juliette protested.

"He did."

"When?"

"Before your time. I assume your development stopped when your earthly body died. But even with the mind of a twenty-one-year-old, you should be able to understand that your position comes with great responsibility. Don't be petty about what happened to you on Earth."

"Petty! My life was cut short! You might think it's petty to be angry about that, but for those of us born and raised on this filthy planet, we have only one life. Taking a life is not petty!" Juliette cried.

"So what exactly are you trying to do with Ciaran?"

"He's mine!" Juliette looked like a child having a temper tantrum, like she wanted to stomp her feet in anger. But she was able to refrain from doing so.

Ayana shook her head. "You're still a child, and I am afraid you'll never grow up." Ayana waved her arms in the air. The air pressure crushed Juliette's hologram. She heaved and hissed in anger.

"You don't have the power to exile me."

"Maybe not. But I can certainly constrain all of your power."

"No, you can't!" Juliette yelled.

A spark of white light cut through the air, and the hologram of Richard Kelley appeared.

"We need her," he said. "You can't do this Ayana."

Madeline called out from outside the light circle, "Grandfather!"

"He comes for you, doesn't he? Well, I won't let him take you." Ciaran stood up, pulling Madeline away. He could hardly walk. Each movement he made felt like he was trying to move a mountain.

Madeline wrapped her arm around his waist to support him. Tadgh was right behind. They rushed toward the car.

Inside the wind circle, Ayana crushed Juliette harder. Juliette's hologram looked as if it was disintegrating. Richard then swung his white sword and broke through the air pressure around Juliette.

"You need Juliette to balance your power, don't you? You're selfish, Richard."

Richard sneered. "We have no real leadership now. If I don't take care of my power, who will?"

"Eudaiz is a place for everyone. You don't have to overpower the council. The thirty-three-year cycle has come. We will have a new leader."

"No, Ayana. If we can't get stronger, we'll be ruined. I can't let you restrain Juliette."

"She will be the one who ruins us. Every day Ciaran is still on this planet, we're vulnerable. And yet all she can see is her petty resentment."

"But she's a certainty. He's not." Richard pointed at Ciaran. "I'm taking Juliette with me." He approached Juliette.

"You underestimate me, Richard." Ayana turned toward Madeline and waved her arm.

Madeline slumped to the ground and covered her ears. "That jingle, that sound again," she said. It was the same sound she had heard from Mrs.

Hanson and the Roman soldiers. It was a sound that made her head feel like it was exploding. And now it was coming from Ayana.

Ciaran grabbed her. He helped to cover her ears, but it didn't seem to help at all. Madeline's nose started to bleed.

Ciaran charged back toward the tornado. "Ayana, tell me what you want and I'll do it."

Ciaran couldn't penetrate the wind wall. He stood there, helpless.

Richard tightened his grip on his sword. Ayana cocked an eyebrow at him in challenge. "Juliette or Madeline. Choose."

"Richard, Madeline is your granddaughter!" Ciaran shouted at Richard.

"You don't know anything, Ciaran."

"Your ally or your granddaughter, Richard?" Ayana said dryly, her face as cold as steel.

Richard turned toward Madeline. "Madeline, I now name you the successor of Sciphil One. Do you accept?"

"Accept what?" Madeline puffed out the question.

Ayana's composure wavered slightly. It was surprise and anger that Ciaran saw on her face. He recalled Ayana telling Juliette before that she could not hurt a successor. It could work. Although they might be jumping out of the frying pan and into the fire, he didn't have any other solution at the moment.

Ciaran staggered back, kneeling next to Madeline. Tadgh cradled her in his arms. She was fading. Blood came out of her nose and trickled from her mouth.

"Madeline, they can't hurt a successor of whatever it was he said. Just accept it. Please," Ciaran said.

"Are you sure her soul is virtuous?" Ayana said.

"I'm sure," Richard said. "She lived on this bloody planet, and she works as a journalist. Her soul is probably like a nun's by this point, which is very unfortunate."

"What the hell does that mean?" Ciaran asked.

"A virtuous soul belongs to someone who has never killed an innocent. If her soul isn't virtuous, succeeding a Sciphil position will only kill her," Ayana said, casting a glance at Madeline, who was on the verge of passing out.

"I need you to stay alive. Please just say yes." Ciaran wiped the blood from her face. His hands shook uncontrollably. He wasn't sure if he shook more because he was weakened or because he feared losing her.

"I can't lose you, Madeline. Accept whatever it is. We will work out the next step," he said.

She closed her eyes.

"No, Madeline, don't leave me. Don't do this to me. Just say yes."

The world was a blur to Ciaran. Blood was everywhere. His blood. Her blood. He didn't know which was which. He grabbed Madeline from Tadgh and held her in his arms. "Please."

Richard repeated, "My granddaughter, I name you as the successor of Sciphil One. Do you accept?"

Ciaran hadn't a shred of strength left in him, but he would fight until he was sure she survived. He held her in his arms and waited.

Then, to his relief, she nodded. "Yes, I accept."

Ayana withdrew the sound wave immediately. She moved close to the wind wall without stepping outside and said dryly, "I hope it's worth it, Ciaran. Remember, the day you accept the responsibility, many lives are in your hands. So choose your actions very carefully." She turned and disappeared as quickly as she had appeared.

"Which position? What am I responsible for?" Ciaran asked, although he knew Ayana was gone and couldn't hear him.

Richard grabbed Juliette, and they both disappeared along with the tornado.

The chilly cemetery returned to its eerie quietness. In front of Madeline, Ciaran, and Tadgh was a scene from a war zone.

Madeline recovered soon after the sound stopped. Ciaran spat out more blood. The surgical wound on his chest continued to bleed. He stood up and staggered back toward the destroyed tomb.

On the platform, Juliette's coffin was open. The inside was empty. He wasn't hallucinating. The body hadn't just blown away in the wind. The interior of the coffin appeared to be completely intact.

Juliette's body had never been inside the coffin.

Ciaran glanced around in shock. What had happened to his world? Then it dawned on him. His mother had opened Mon Ciel's security shield once, an impossible task to do by herself. There were only two people with the access code to the shield—himself and his father.

Ciaran scrambled toward his father's grave, which had also been blown open by Juliette's tornado. His father's coffin was not just empty—it had obviously been without a body inside for twenty years.

He stood completely still for a moment. It seemed as though the ground was shifting under his feet. He turned and left the tomb floor. He stumbled toward Madeline as she ran to him, reaching him just as he passed out cold on the ground.

CHAPTER 5

The world gradually came back to Ciaran as he opened his eyes. Ayana's voice still echoed in his head, *"Are you sure her soul is virtuous?"* Ciaran wasn't sure if he had forced Madeline into a dead end. He was a bit afraid of another one of Juliette's scenarios.

Had Madeline killed before? he wondered.

It wasn't just any killing, but the killing of an innocent that he worried about. He couldn't see signs of such violence in her. But if she had killed someone, surely she wouldn't have accepted what Richard had offered.

Ciaran gazed at the ceiling of his bedroom at Mon Ciel for a few minutes to regain his bearings. Suddenly, his view was pleasantly obstructed by the gorgeous green eyes of Jo looking at him.

"Hey, White Knight, you're back!" She grinned and slid her arm underneath his back to help him sit up in his bed. It surprised Ciaran how strong Jo was given her petite physique.

"How's your shoulder, Jo?"

She shifted the shoulder that had been dislocated during the fight at Fountains Abbey and smiled. "See? No need for a sling. Let me get you some water."

She got up to get the water from a jug sitting on the side table.

Ciaran took the glass of water. "Thanks. Where's Madeline?"

"Down at the library, talking things over with Tadgh. Strategies. Important matters. Things that happened at the cemetery."

Ciaran nodded.

"Aren't you thirsty?" Jo pointed at the glass of water that he still held in his hand.

Ciaran laughed. "I know they asked you to drug me when I woke up. But you'll have to be a bit more subtle than that to fool me, Jo."

"Damn it," Jo muttered.

He turned the glass of water around in a circle. "How long have you known Madeline?"

"As long as I can remember. I think we met at school. Why do you ask?"

Ciaran smiled. "You're Madeline's friend. I'd just like to get to know you a bit more."

"You want to know me? Or Madeline?"

Ciaran chuckled. "Both. Do you like Tadgh?"

Jo sat down at his bedside, looked straight into his eyes, and answered without even the slightest squirm, "He's not my type."

Ciaran nodded. *She didn't even sugarcoat it.* Jo intrigued him. Strong-minded. Strong-willed. Just the type that would stupefy his brother. Ciaran shifted his body to get off the bed. Jo stood up, hands on her hips.

"I wasn't able to drug you, but I'm very sure I can knock you out. Lie down, Ciaran."

Ciaran smiled. "I need to get to my computer. It's very important."

"Can't let you. Doctor's orders."

"Or Madeline's?"

"Same thing. She can be pretty scary when she's pissed off."

"All right. Here's the deal. You either let me work on my computer or simply answer my questions. Then I won't need to move."

Jo bit her pouting bottom lip. "As long as the questions aren't too tricky, shoot."

"Does Madeline have a criminal record?"

Jo laughed. "No."

"Does she have any record of committing violence against others?"

"Of course not. Give her a white dress, and she'd turn into Cinderella. Or a nun. Why are you asking? Honestly?"

"What about off the record? I'm asking for your opinion here."

The smile faded from Jo's face. She stared at Ciaran and said nothing.

"I love her. You know that by now. Do you think I'd do anything to harm her?"

Jo shook her head. "I know you wouldn't. But it's not you that I'm worried about. It's Madeline herself."

His blood ran cold, and fear pounded in his head. He was suddenly afraid that his gut instinct had been right, that it couldn't be as easy as making a promise to be a successor of Sciphil One to solve the problem Ayana had presented.

"I don't know. I want to know the answer to that, too," Jo said.

"Why, Jo?"

"Because I want to know if I was responsible for making her do the unthinkable. I can't make her talk. Why don't you try, Ciaran? Ask her what happened in Australia ten years ago."

"You think she might have killed someone?"

"As I said, I don't know what happened. I was there with her. And when I woke up, those people were dead."

"Why do you think you'd be responsible if Madeline killed them?"

He stood up to go to the computer. Jo didn't stop him this time. "Don't bother looking up the records, Ciaran. There's nothing to find. I wiped it. That was the only time I hacked into any system."

He turned around and looked at Jo. There was the gleam of tears in her eyes, but she didn't let any fall.

"I'm sorry about what happened to you, Jo. And I'm sorry I had to ask about it."

Ciaran reached out to embrace her, but she stepped back. She looked him square in the eye. "The man was trying to rape me. He knocked me unconscious. When I came to, it was already over. Everyone was dead, and Madeline was there. So ask her if she killed them because of me. I need to know."

She couldn't hold back any longer, and tears rolled down her face. "Everything was burned to the ground. All Madeline told me was that there had been an accident, and she only had enough time to drag me out. But I know she was lying."

"I'll ask . . ."

Suddenly the migraine hit him in a tremendous wave. Ciaran grabbed his head and slumped to the floor. A distant voice pierced his mind, stabbing his brain like shards of glass. He'd heard this voice before, but this time it wasn't the usual robotic monotone voice. It was one with an Irish accent.

"We're finally connected, Ciaran," it said. "It's about time you come back to us to fulfill your duty."

"Who are you?" Ciaran asked. The person didn't seem to hear his question. The static noise continued, and the voice kept ranting.

"Thirty-three years I've been waiting, Ciaran. It's time."

The voice was so distorted that Ciaran couldn't make sense of what he was trying to say.

Jo held Ciaran's shoulders. "Ciaran, look at me. Ciaran . . . Take this water . . . Who are you talking to?"

"Speak clearer," said Ciaran. "I can't hear you, goddamnit. What is Sciphil? What does Madeline have to do with any of this?"

"Madeline . . . Madeline . . . she's the key . . ." The voice faded away.

"No, no! Don't go! What's Sciphil?" His vision was blurry. He tried to hang on to the sound of the voice as much as possible, but it seemed to have gone completely away.

"You're bleeding, Ciaran." Jo wiped the blood that trickled from his nose. "Not another Sciphil. I have had enough of this . . ."

Ciaran blinked. "What did you just say, Jo?"

CHAPTER 6

Ciaran punched the call button on the intercom in his office. A short moment later, Tadgh and Madeline appeared at the door. Ciaran looked at Madeline. His views about her had changed. Much more than the woman he loved, in front of him stood a world of secrets that he had to explore.

Madeline cocked an eyebrow at Jo, who was sitting comfortably with a laptop on a reading chair. "I tried to drug him, but he figured it out," Jo said in response to Madeline's look.

Ciaran smiled and gestured to the table and chair in the far corner where they could sit. Tadgh frowned.

"Are you okay to be up and about? I'll call Doctor Thomas, Ciaran."

"You can pull a better threat than that, Tadgh. Coffee anyone?"

"I'll have one, please," Madeline said.

Ciaran went to the coffee machine. "I told Jo about what happened at the cemetery. We need to decipher a few puzzles before we can plan any strategies to deal with the problem at hand. What's a Sciphil, and what does being a successor mean?" Ciaran sat down on the sofa with a tray of coffee for everyone.

He served Madeline her coffee, resting his gaze on her face for a brief moment before continuing. "Jo heard of the term Sciphil way before us."

"A couple of months ago, my friend, Zach, asked me if I knew what a Sciphil was. He never told me where he came across the word. He asked me because he thought it had to do with hologame technology. He's a player, not a designer, and he didn't know the technical aspects of the game. I didn't have an answer for Zach and really didn't think much about it."

"Maybe I should talk to him," Ciaran said.

"I don't think that's necessary. If he knew, he wouldn't have asked Jo," Madeline said.

Ciaran noticed Madeline shift in her chair. She looked uncomfortable with the idea. "I just want to know how he came across the concept. But first things first, we should be safe from Sciphils if we stay inside Mon Ciel. My father designed its shield to protect us," Ciaran said.

"Is that the same shield you used to put Mon Ciel on lockdown before?" Madeline asked.

Ciaran shook his head. "No. That was an emergency lockdown. Mon Ciel's energy lock is permanent. To put it simply, it locks anything carrying extraterrestrial energy out of this place."

Tadgh grabbed his coffee and dropped two sugar cubes in it. When he reached for a third, Ciaran smacked his hand away. Tadgh grumbled some profanity and withdrew. "All Father told me was that if we had any problems, we should just stay inside Mon Ciel." Tadgh sipped his coffee. "Like sheep."

"I've seen Ayana before. I remember her," Ciaran said.

"The woman at the cemetery?" Madeline asked.

Ciaran nodded. "Father and Mother took me outside Mon Ciel's fence to see Ayana and a man. I was only two or thereabouts because Mother had just had Tadgh. The man said something to me that I didn't quite understand. But then he gave me a golden toy and asked if I liked it. I must have said yes and taken the toy because I thought it would look nice dangling on his cot." Ciaran shot a glance at Tadgh.

"Is that what the woman meant by you have agreed to be a bloody successor? If that's the case, it hardly qualifies as a consent," Tadgh exclaimed and snatched a cube of sugar, popping it in his mouth before Ciaran could stop him.

Ciaran shook his head at Tadgh. "Anyway, Father argued with the man, and Mother took me and ran inside. The man and Ayana tried to chase her, but they stopped just before the fence."

"They couldn't get through the shield!" Tadgh said.

Ciaran nodded. "We never talked about the incident again, and I soon forgot about it. I can ask Mother for more information."

Tadgh shook his head. "I just got a voice message saying she's fine. She has something to do and will get back to us when she's done. I tried to return the call, but it didn't work."

Ciaran reached his hand out. "Give me your phone. I'll trace the number."

Tadgh shrugged and gave the cell phone to Ciaran. "It's weird. She's never done this before."

Ciaran looked at the message, entered some codes, and stared at the small screen of the phone. "She didn't use the standard telecommunication technology. These are frequency signals," Ciaran muttered and pulled out his cell phone.

He retrieved the message Sciphil Two had sent to his cell phone last week then entered a string of code into his phone and looked up at everyone. "Sciphil Two used the same type of frequency."

"We talked to Sciphil Two's people in the basement at Mrs. Hanson's place. We might have to go back there to get the equipment," Jo said.

Ciaran nodded. "Yes. We have equipment here, but to get the right communication frequency, we'll have to go back." He stood up.

"Where do you think you're going?" Tadgh asked. "What if Juliette comes back? Can you handle another round of tornado wrestling?"

"Can you handle *one?* Guns won't work on whatever it is out there that's using Juliette's form," Ciaran said.

Tadgh laughed. "You still don't believe that that thing is Juliette?"

Ciaran sat down and leaned back in his chair. "Juliette is clinically dead. And it's not a statement made out of sentiment, Tadgh. What we saw was a collective of energy, a simulated form based on Juliette's psychological and biological profile when she was alive."

"In layman's terms, we call it a spirit. A ghost," Madeline deadpanned and sipped her coffee.

"I know a ghost is not a viable scientific explanation, Ciaran. But a simulated profile in a hologame requires someone to design and control it. Apart from you being one of the very few people on this planet who can do that, to make it happen, the person has to have an intimate knowledge of Juliette's profile. Unless . . ." Jo blinked her big green eyes, expecting Ciaran to understand and complete her sentence.

Ciaran nodded. "Unless Juliette's brain is still alive, and she is creating the profile herself. Given her body is not where it is supposed to be, I'd say it's a plausible explanation, Jo."

Tadgh sneered. "I'd buy Madeline's ghost's theory before that!" He shook his head. "Regardless, I'll go to Mrs. Hanson's place to get the machine for you. Whatever Juliette is, she wants you, not me. And you stay here, too, Madeline. Richard wants you, and until we figure all this out, leaving Mon Ciel isn't a good idea."

Ciaran arched an eyebrow and chuckled to himself as he watched his brother take charge.

Jo stood up. "Let's go," she said. "You don't know how to pack up a computer system properly—apart from pulling the plugs and stuffing the pieces into boxes. If the equipment is damaged, there's no way we can communicate with the person or being that we need to talk to."

Ciaran chuckled. Tadgh shrugged and turned on his heel. Madeline grabbed Jo's shoulder. "Be careful, Jo."

"Don't worry, Madeline. I'm more capable than you think." Jo smiled and followed Tadgh out.

When Tadgh and Jo had left, Madeline started to follow, but Ciaran grabbed her elbow, pulling her into his arms.

"They know their way out." He smiled.

"Do they?" Madeline played with Ciaran's hair. "How's the pain?"

"Fine." He kissed the dimple on her left cheek. Then he moved to her lips. She didn't let the kiss go deeper.

"Let me." Madeline unbuttoned the top of his shirt and examined the bandage that Doctor Thomas had secured to Ciaran's chest. Satisfied that the wound was not bleeding, she redid the buttons.

Then she checked the big gash on his arm and the swollen tattoo of the golden crucifix.

"From this angle, the crucifix looks like a key," Madeline said.

"From my angle, it looks like a cocktail spoon." Ciaran grabbed her chin, lifting it up. "Why are you avoiding looking at me?"

"I'm not." She turned toward the window.

Ciaran turned her face back to him. There were tears in her eyes. He kissed her big brown eyes. "Ayana mentioned the consequence of not having a virtuous soul when accepting the successor role with your grandfather. I'm not questioning you. But I'm asking you to tell me honestly whether or not I should let you go through with the promise."

She eased away from his hold. "It's *my* promise . . ."

"No, it's *our* promise. You're an important part of my life now. You know all about me, so you don't get to reveal only some information to me and withhold the rest. Why were you uncomfortable when Jo mentioned Zach? What happened in Australia ten years ago, Madeline?"

Tears gleamed in her eyes now. "I need time to think about this."

He wiped the tears and kissed her. "An hour. I can't bear any longer than that. I need to know."

A loud bang echoed through the house. It didn't shake the building, but they could feel the vibrations in the air. Ciaran darted to the window. From the sky, beams of light struck Mon Ciel but disintegrated and vanished into thin air.

"Whoever that is couldn't penetrate the shield," Ciaran muttered.

Amid the disintegrated beams of light, a gigantic image of Juliette appeared, glowing in a white and blue halo. She smiled at Ciaran. A flash of amusement crossed her face. She hit Mon Ciel again with the light beams then turned on her heel and moved away because her beams were unable to damage the premises.

"Tadgh!" Ciaran said and rushed toward the coffee table to grab his cell phone. He called Tadgh and heard only the endless sound of static from the other end of the line.

CHAPTER 7

"All right, just to be clear, I'll talk to the cops. If things get complicated, we walk. Okay?" said Tadgh. He parked a block away from Mrs. Hanson's house. They had driven past earlier and could see police vehicles, flashing lights, and a crowd of people flooding that end of the street. He wagered walking right through the police's front line wouldn't be a good idea.

Jo rolled her eyes and stomped forward. Tadgh looked at her fragile figure on heels. "How do you walk on those sticks?"

Jo whirled around. "They're called high heels—a girl's most precious and lethal weapon. Don't you make me use them on you. They might cause some permanent damage to your reproductive ability."

Tadgh shook his head and escorted her as they approached the house.

Mrs. Hanson's house had been sealed off again. Police were everywhere, carrying out boxes of evidence. Among the boxes, Tadgh and Jo recognized the equipment from the basement they needed.

Tadgh wrapped his arm around Jo's shoulders and approached the officer standing at the barricades.

"Hi, officer. What's going on here?" Tadgh shot a concerned look at the unfriendly officer.

"This is a crime scene. Civilians shouldn't be here."

"This is Jo's grandmother's house. She's visiting from the US. Surely you can tell us what's going on. She's quite worried."

The officer glanced at Jo. "Who's your grandmother?"

"Mrs. Hanson."

"Can I see your ID please, ma'am?"

"Sure."

Jo reached for her purse. "Damn it. All my documentation is in the travel packet. I left it at the hotel. Look, officer, I just landed. I want to see my grandmother. Can you please tell me what's going on here?"

"We can go back to the hotel and get the papers for you," said Tadgh. "But can you at least tell her what happened? Is Mrs. Hanson okay?"

Jo squeezed out a fake tear.

Seeing Jo's tear, the officer shifted his stance and cleared his throat. "Ma'am, I can't tell you much because I don't know who you are. But I'm sorry to say that it's not good news regarding Mrs. Hanson."

Jo manufactured some more tears and looked as if she was about to make a fuss. "What do you mean? I want to go inside. I want to see her."

"Ma'am, if you wait here, I'll go and get the captain for you . . ."

The police carried a couple of body bags from the house.

"Oh my God." Jo pointed. "Is that her, in a body bag? Why are there two? She lived here by herself."

Jo pushed at the barricades. Tadgh helped. "What the hell is going on here?" Tadgh said.

"Stay back, stay back. Don't cause me any trouble, ma'am. Mrs. Hanson died a few weeks ago. That isn't her body."

"What? Died? So whose bodies are those? My other relatives?" Jo kept pushing.

"Ma'am, stay still. Ma'am. We're busy here. There are forty bodies in there. If you claim they're your relatives, I'll go and get the captain." The officer was beginning to get angry.

Jo nodded. "Please. I'll stay here."

As soon as the officer disappeared inside the house, Tadgh and Jo ran, vanishing into the dark.

"Someone must have shifted all the soldiers' bodies from Fountains Abbey to here," Tadgh said while they were running. Jo stumbled on a tree branch. Tadgh snatched her up and carried her in his arms.

"Let go of me. I can run on my own."

"The evidence points to the contrary," Tadgh muttered and kept going. He got to the car and deposited Jo in the passenger seat. She slapped his shoulder when he got into the driver's seat.

Tadgh reached over and pinned Jo's arms down. His face hovered right next to hers. "I said, let *me* handle the talking. What exactly didn't you understand about that? What if the cops got you? What I would do then?" he growled.

"I didn't do anything wrong to be afraid of the cops."

"You might not have. But our family is not exactly cop friendly. So when you're with us, keep that in mind."

"I'm not *with* you . . . nobody tells me what to do . . ."

Then he kissed her. It seemed to be the only way to stop her from talking. Or maybe he just wanted to do it. Whatever the reason, he did it.

Tadgh eased off. "I expected a slap in the face," he said.

Jo rolled her eyes. "I'm sure it's illegal to resort to such violence for a pathetic kiss."

"Pathetic? I risked my skin doing that, and all I've got is—"

Jo hopped up and kissed him.

A wave of passionate energy washed over him. Tadgh considered himself to be experienced, but the energy coming from Jo was irresistible. Every bone and muscle in his body seemed to liquefy.

Jo finished the kiss and sat back in her seat.

"How's that? If you're going to risk your skin doing something like that, you should do it properly," she said and buckled her seatbelt.

"I'll try better next time," Tadgh muttered and started the car.

As Tadgh drove out, lightning slashed across the sky, and thunder rumbled around them. A wind came up suddenly, crashing through the trees on the street and shaking loose the shingles on a few of the small cottage roofs along the road. The funnel of spinning air was headed straight toward Mrs. Hanson's house.

"This is not a normal storm. It's Juliette," Tadgh said. "In other words, we're fucked." He accelerated, forgetting all about his speed phobia.

They hadn't gone far before the car hit something and spun around. The car rolled, smashed into a tree trunk, and stopped. All of the interior airbags went off. One headlight still beamed out into the misted air. Tadgh unfastened his seatbelt and reached over to Jo. "Are you okay?"

"Yep." Jo wriggled her way out from behind the airbag, and they both climbed out of the car.

It was a dark night. No stars. No moon. No street lights.

Jo grabbed Tadgh's hand. "Run!"

"We can't. It's too late. Juliette is here already!"

CHAPTER 8

A body thudded into the mud right behind them, splashing rain water onto the wet grass. Tadgh and Jo turned around to see Stefan's dead body on the ground.

A beam of light appeared, and the holographic image of Juliette swung back and forth as if not sure whether to fly away or stay.

"He's unfixable," Juliette growled, looking at Stefan's dead body.

"Apparently!" Tadgh stepped in front of Jo. "What do you want?"

The hologram turned toward Tadgh. "I want your brother of course!"

"And you think you can capture me and lure Ciaran out here? You and your dead brother were scamming Ciaran for years. Did that get you anything?"

Juliette swung her arm up. Tadgh's body lifted, spun around, and was flung down to the ground.

Tadgh grunted with pain and stood up. "Overreacting a little, don't you think?"

Juliette's face had lost all of what Ciaran had once loved. In front of Tadgh was a demon to the core. Tadgh didn't know what had caused this change. He wasn't sure whether the real Juliette was still alive or not. Her body wasn't in her coffin. He had no idea what to make of this situation. But what he did know was that the demon standing in front of him wanted Ciaran, and it would kill to get what it wanted.

This was no ghost. The thing standing in front of Tadgh was real. It wasn't solid because it was a hologram. But it certainly was no spirit seeking revenge.

"You." Juliette pointed at Jo. "Go back and tell Ciaran to come and claim his brother."

"I . . . I don't drive . . . I'm sorry. And besides, you trashed the car."

That was such a lie, Tadgh thought.

"Want to fly?" The air around Juliette started to stir as she spoke.

"Oh, no, no!" Tadgh waved Juliette off. There was no way Jo's fragile body could survive the impact that Ciaran had suffered this morning. "You'll kill her. A dead messenger is no good to you."

Tadgh didn't know what to do, but he was willing to try anything. He pulled out his phone. "I could call him. But, unfortunately, you and your weird energy kills all the phone signals."

Juliette smiled. "All right. I can keep my distance," she said and stepped back.

Tadgh dialed. "Yep . . . sure . . . yes . . . cemetery? What?" Tadgh looked around. "Yeah, the cemetery. The second one of the day. Yep, that's where I am."

Juliette raised an eyebrow in question.

Tadgh shrugged. "What? Phones these days have Bluetooth signals and map tracking. You think I need to shout out the exact address?"

"Stay here and run when you can, okay?" Tadgh mumbled to Jo.

"I'm not going to leave you."

"I don't want to have to protect you. Go when I say so."

Tadgh approached Juliette. "I saw your coffin this morning. There was no body in it. What happened to you?"

Juliette snorted. "When will Ciaran be here?"

"Half an hour. He's not flying . . . He chose to drive."

Juliette smirked. "You like her?" She nodded toward Jo.

"She's all right. She obviously doesn't compare to you, Juliette."

Juliette laughed. "Sorry, darling. I love one man, and one man only. And that's your brother. I think you're a good man, Tadgh." Juliette glanced at Jo. "You're lucky. He likes you."

"He's not exactly my type," said Jo.

"Look, there's no point keeping her here. Let her go," Tadgh said.

Juliette shrugged. "All right. Sure. But you're waiting here with me, Tadgh."

"No, I'll stay," Jo stated firmly.

"Well now." Juliette cast a warm look at Jo. "You *do* like him."

"I'd do that for any friend. I have faith in people. I don't scam and cheat those I care for."

Juliette's face turned red.

"Oh, no. Let's calm down, ladies," Tadgh suggested.

He reached out his hand to grab Juliette and felt a jolt of energy. A substance. Tadgh got closer to Juliette. He looked into her eyes. Juliette looked up at him. Tadgh knew he had a few of the same characteristics as Ciaran. He stepped closer. So close it was almost intimate. He reached his hand up.

"May I?"

Juliette looked as if she had tears in her eyes.

Tadgh touched her face. There was something there. Not flesh. But energy. It felt solid.

"What does my brother have that I don't?"

Juliette looked at Tadgh as if she wanted to devour his face. "Not much. You have everything Ciaran has. He just happened to come first."

Tadgh smiled. He gently slid his hand toward the back of her neck. He could feel her tremble. Tadgh touched his lips to hers. There was a feeling of contact. He deepened the kiss. He could feel her body pressed against him. Tadgh caressed Juliette, moving his hand down her back and to her hip. Then as quick as lightning, he pulled the dagger from her side. His right arm still holding her tight, Tadgh stabbed Juliette with his left. He pulled the dagger out and stabbed again for good measure.

Juliette staggered back, hissing in anger and pain. The thick smell of burning electrical current filled the air. Something sparked underneath her skin.

Tadgh yelled at Jo, "Run!"

Instead of running away, Jo rushed toward Tadgh. She grabbed a tree branch and whacked at Juliette.

The holographic figure was distorted severely as the branch went through it. It hissed and screamed.

Tadgh stabbed again. This time, he aimed at Juliette's heart.

Her holographic figure suddenly stood straight. It poked its chest out to take the dagger. Then it laughed. It grabbed Tadgh's hand twisted his arm, and flung him away.

Tadgh hit a tree and fell to the ground. He moaned and stood up, leaning against the tree. Jo darted toward him. She picked up another tree branch and stood in front of Tadgh protectively while Juliette approached them.

"I told you to run," Tadgh said.

"Shut up."

"I don't need your protection."

"Sorry to tread so heavily on your manhood. But you're going to have to let us girls fight it out."

Jo wouldn't stand a chance with Juliette one-on-one, Tadgh thought.

Juliette approached slowly, like a leopard playing with its dying prey.

"Run, please. I'll keep her here," Tadgh said.

"You can't be a hero. And you can certainly choose not be an idiot."

Juliette raised her arm. Tadgh had no idea what was coming, but he knew it was going to be bad. Tadgh and Jo felt the air pressure coming from Juliette. There would be an explosion. They would be dead very soon.

Juliette smirked and was about to swing her arm.

Tadgh grabbed Jo from behind. He turned her around and kissed her. Long and deep. He had to match what she had done before. A man had his pride, after all. If they were going to die, this was something he had to do.

Something exploded behind them. But they didn't feel anything. Surprised and confused, Tadgh and Jo opened their eyes.

In front of them stood a man in his late sixties with a sword in his hand. The sword blade glowed bright orange. Juliette grabbed her right shoulder, which was dripping with blood.

"You grew strong fast, Sciphil Nine."

"You have three seconds to disappear," the man said dryly.

Juliette cast a last hateful look at Tadgh and whirled away, disappearing into the darkness.

Tadgh stood still, bracing himself with one hand on the tree trunk, measuring the man with his eyes as he approached them. He was as tall as Tadgh. His salt and peppered hair was slightly long and tied back, revealing kind eyes. He looked Tadgh up and down.

"You're a strong man, Tadgh. You'd make a good warrior. Is your brother as strong as you are?"

"Stronger. Are you stronger than Juliette? Tell us how we can fight her."

The man laughed. "The LeBlanc boys live up to their reputation."

The old man turned around and walked away so fast that Tadgh didn't have time to ask another question. Unlike Juliette, who had simply disappeared, this man walked away at an impossible speed.

Standing in the quietness of the night, Jo asked, "You didn't call Ciaran, did you?"

"No. I was just pretending . . ."

"So what's that then?" Jo asked and pointed toward car headlights flashing in their direction.

CHAPTER 9

Madeline followed Ciaran as he bolted to the fence line of Mon Ciel as soon as security cleared Lindsay's car.

She was anxious about Jo and Tadgh, but her psychic mind was telling her they were unharmed. Ciaran had no psychic ability. Regardless of what she had told him, the short hour had dragged like a torturous decade for him. He was worried sick about what might have happened to Tadgh and Jo.

Madeline yanked the car door open on Jo's side. Jo hopped out.

"I'm all right," she said and rushed to Tadgh's side. Tadgh pushed the door open. "I can get out of the car myself, lady!" he muttered and wobbled out.

"What's the problem, Tadgh?" Ciaran asked.

"Nothing," Tadgh snapped.

"He twisted his ankle," Jo said.

"I landed wrong. That's all. And I can certainly speak for myself," he grumbled.

"I appreciate this, Lindsay," Ciaran said when his assistant stepped out of the car.

Madeline knew Lindsay was more than Ciaran's right-hand man. They were friends. After losing Robert, it had taken a lot out of Ciaran to call Lindsay to handle this task. From the corner of her eye, Madeline saw a blue dot just outside the fence. It hovered there, trying to catch her attention.

She was sure it wasn't Juliette. Juliette's blue dots would be inside Mon Ciel because she knew better than anyone that the shield didn't work against thoughts and humans, only against extraterrestrial energy. Whoever waited out there wanting to talk to her might never have entered Mon Ciel before.

She glanced back just before entering the house and saw the blue dot had grown larger. She could hear a clear voice now. "This is Ayana, Madeline. If you want to know exactly what you and Ciaran have gotten yourselves into, come outside Mon Ciel, and we'll talk."

Madeline wanted to respond, but she didn't know how. She could trace thoughts and could see them, but she had never interacted with them before. Speaking out loud wasn't a good idea—that much she knew.

She closed her eyes. Concentrated. She willed her response into her mind and sent her stream of thought toward Ayana. "You want me to go out there so you can beat the hell out of me again?"

"I withdrew my attack on you as soon as you'd given your consent to the Sciphil One successor position. No harm from me will ever come to you again."

Madeline smiled to herself. Her communication channel with these extraterrestrial people actually worked. *Wish I'd known this before and saved Tadgh and Jo the trip*, she thought privately. "What about others like Juliette? Will they respect the rules as you do?"

"I can't speak for others. I have a vested interest in Ciaran staying alive. I think you do, too. Come alone, and we will sort this out."

"Why can't you tell Ciaran directly?"

"I sealed his Sciphil successor position at the cemetery. That connected him directly to our communication network. Any message to him at my level will be recorded. Your psychic ability is unique, but I'm not sure how long it will be before it is intercepted. We need to speak face-to-face if you care for him. I promise you my protection."

"Damn it. Okay. I'll see what I can do."

"Do what?" Ciaran asked.

She opened her eyes and realized she had spoken the last sentence out loud. "Find a different way to talk to those Sciphils," she said.

She smiled at him. She tucked a strand of stray hair on his face back and looked into his intense gray eyes that had lost some of their shine due to fatigue. Still, he was too beautiful for her to stare at for a long time without losing her control and telling him whatever was on her mind. She reached up and kissed him.

"I told you Tadgh and Jo would be fine."

"You were right. Let's get inside before you catch a cold." He wrapped his arm around her shoulder to take her inside the house.

The warmth of his body and the virility in his aura made her want to curl up in his arms and live there for the next millennium. She wished she could forget the conversation she'd just had with Ayana.

Jo was waiting for them in the hallway. She gave Ciaran a small electronic pad. "I made this. It's a portable game console for beginners. Could you give it to Tadgh? With his wrecked ankle, I think he has to lie still for a while. I don't want his brains to turn to mush from boredom."

"I'll fix his ankle now, and he will be chasing you around in an hour. But the game console is a nice idea. Why don't you give it to him yourself?"

"We don't talk anymore. He's like a petulant child."

Ciaran took the game from Jo. "All right."

Madeline could see a flash of intrigue in Ciaran's eyes. *He very much approves of Jo and Tadgh together.* "Can I have a word with you, Jo?" she asked.

"Sure."

"I'll fix Tadgh up now. And I'm still going to make him play this game." Ciaran smiled and strode away.

Madeline waited until Ciaran disappeared around the corner of the seemingly endless marble corridor. She turned to Jo and found her friend observing her with questions in her cat green eyes. Her long black hair cascaded down the sides of her foxy face. She was focused on Madeline.

"Secret talk?" Jo asked.

"What a trip! I just want to calm you down."

Jo snorted. "You think I'm in need of your soothing therapy?"

Madeline shook her head. "Maybe not. Maybe it's just an excuse for some quiet time."

Jo laughed. "That's better."

"You like Tadgh, Jo."

Jo shrugged. "Perhaps. It's weird, though, because he's not my usual type."

Madeline nodded. "Zach is more your type."

Jo giggled. "He's every girl's type, except yours."

Madeline glanced at the door. Through its small glass panel, she could see the blue dot still hovering outside Mon Ciel. "Next time you talk to Zach, could you tell him that what happened in Australia wasn't his fault?"

Jo narrowed her eyes.

"Don't ask, Jo. Please. Just for once."

"For once? You've never told *me* what happened. I didn't even know that Zach had been feeling guilty. People died in that house, Madeline. And I wiped all records of our involvement. Don't you think I'm entitled to know what happened?"

"I told you it was an accident. The house caught on fire."

"Accident how?" Jo waved her arms in frustration.

"We fought in the kitchen. Larry felt onto a knife, and the house caught on fire. I told you."

"That's lame, Madeline. You're telling me that Larry and his entire family fell onto knives? That wouldn't even make a believable black comedy. I was stupid enough to wipe the record, so I effectively gagged myself. But come on!" Jo stomped around the corridor.

"Look, Jo, I'll tell you more—but later. All I need you to promise me is that you'll tell Zach what I asked you to. I don't want him to live his whole life in doubt. I wasn't sure before. But I'm sure now. It wasn't his fault."

"Why can't you tell him yourself? What are you trying to do, Madeline?"

"All right. I'll tell him myself. Maybe tomorrow. But I want to tell Ciaran first."

Jo nodded. "And when will you tell me the truth?"

"Tomorrow," she stated as firmly as possible.

"I'll hold you to that," Jo said and turned on her heel.

Madeline peeked through the glass panel of the door once more and could see the blue dot looming as large as her pilates ball. She turned and headed down the hall toward Ciaran's room.

CHAPTER 10

She found Ciaran in the bedroom looking out the window. She was one hundred percent sure he couldn't see Ayana's blue dot the way she did. She approached him from behind, embraced him, and took the empty glass from his hand.

"Scotch isn't exactly the prescribed medication Doctor Thomas ordered."

Ciaran turned around. He touched the dimple on her left cheek with his thumb. Then he kissed her. She kissed him back.

Outside Mon Ciel, the blue dot now was as enormous as a hot air balloon, glowing a white and blue light. She stared at it.

"What is that?" Ciaran asked and turned to look outside. Then he turned back in, looking at her. "I saw a blue reflection in your eyes. Have you been seeing those blue dots again?"

"What? Oh. No, no." She waved her arm dismissively and moved toward the bed. "You need to take your meds." She grinned and sat down.

"I'm not a sick old man. I don't need drugs."

"Well, I have some activities in mind that I think you might be interested in. But if you don't take your meds, then I could exacerbate your injuries and hurt you even more." She kicked her shoes off and lay back on the two big pillows on the bed. "These activities could be very physically demanding."

Ciaran winked. "Ah, now that's worth consideration."

She smiled and pulled her blouse off in one swift move.

Ciaran strode to the bed as quick as a cat. She swore she heard him purr. "All right, then. Drug me," he said and climbed onto the bed to kiss her. She put her finger on his lips to stop him.

"You know where the meds are," Madeline said.

"I can take them afterward."

She shook her head. "That's not part of the deal."

Ciaran mumbled some words of disagreement, dismounted the bed, and walked toward the cabinet to get the antibiotics and painkillers Doctor Thomas had given him the previous morning. Madeline fetched a glass of water.

Ciaran took the pills and winced. "Now I want serious compensation."

Madeline laughed. "Don't you dare tell me you hate taking medicine! Pharmaceuticals are your bread and butter."

"Medicine is fine when I don't need to take it myself." Ciaran winced again. "I have to tell the lab to make these pills taste better."

Ciaran put the water aside and pulled Madeline into his arms. "Now, how do you plan to reward me?"

Madeline smiled. She pushed at his chest, backing him up toward the bed. He lifted her, and before she knew it, she was lying on her back on the bed. Her pants were on the floor, Ciaran's face was buried between her breasts, and his hands were very busy elsewhere on her body.

Suddenly he slowed down considerably and flopped down, lying on top of her. For the first time, she resented the quality of the LeBlanc's drugs and wished Doctor Thomas had given Ciaran a lighter dose. She gingerly pushed him aside. His voice slurred as he asked, "What's in those meds?"

She turned him so he lay on his back and pulled the blanket up over his chest. She kissed his cheek. "The sedative was in the water. Sleep tight, darling. I love you."

He grabbed her hand. "Don't go," he said. Then his face went totally lax, and he let go of her hand.

She kissed him again, put on her clothes, and grabbed the car keys.

***

Madeline parked the car outside the fence of Mon Ciel and remained in the driver's seat. If things went awry, she would be able to drive straight back inside. Assuring herself that it was a well-planned and justified action, she left the car keys in the ignition and rolled down the window.

Madeline stepped outside the car and waited. Nothing. Maybe this was too close to Mon Ciel. She got into the car and drove slowly down to the creek.

There it was. She could feel it in every cell of her body. The tingle. The energy. Something was coming. Madeline stopped the car and got out.

The air around her thickened. A blue spark zapped through the air, and Ayana appeared. Madeline stepped out of the car and glanced around, staying as close to the car as possible. "First things first . . . what's a Sciphil?"

"You're Richard's successor. It's not my place to give you the induction. He has to train you properly, or you might not pass the Daimon Gate."

"What will happen if I can't get past it?"

"You'll die."

"Can I at least get a dictionary definition of Sciphil?"

"It stands for Scientist Philosopher."

Madeline laughed. "I wouldn't consider myself qualified for either of those positions. Why did Grandfather choose me? Was it because you forced him?"

"If you are not worthy, if your soul is not virtuous, then choosing you is equivalent to giving you a death sentence. Richard has been searching for you for a long time. He has confidence in you. Are you afraid?"

"Does that matter?"

"Yes. Yours was only a promise. You can still deny it if you're not ready. But I have sealed Ciaran's successor position. He can't back out now."

"What the hell does that mean? Does he have to go through the virtuous soul deal like I do?"

"Yes, but it was valid up until the point he gave his consent. And he did that when he was about two years old, Earth time. I think it's a safe bet Bran asked him."

"Who's Bran?"

"The Sciphil that Ciaran is the successor of. I called you out here because Bran's Sciphil position is the most important one and, because of that, many people will want Ciaran dead before he can become a proper Sciphil. To become a Sciphil, he has to pass the Daimon Gate tests, and without training, he has a minimal chance of surviving."

"What if he doesn't follow through with the promise?"

"I told you, his position is sealed." She raised her palm. "The seal has given him more physical strength. But it has also marked his biological profile. If he stays on Earth, he'll die."

"And if he can't pass the Daimon Gate, he'll die, too. Am I right?" Madeline put her hands on her hips.

Ayana nodded.

"So if I want to go with Ciaran through the Daimon Gate, I have to be pretty sure my soul is virtuous. If not, I'll die. If I'm unsure, I can withdraw my promise and live my life on Earth without Ciaran."

Ayana nodded again.

"Do you realize the stupid mess you've just put us in? Who are you, really?"

"My name is Ayana Dee. I am a Sciphil . . ."

"It really doesn't help knowing your name and where you come from. The truth of the matter is . . ." Madeline waved her arms in the air. *Should she even bother elaborating to this alien who doesn't even have a human brain?*

"I want to talk to my grandfather."

"He is too weak to come to you at the moment."

"What?"

"Juliette hurt him. She's changed in the last few weeks. She's no longer conforming to our rules. Richard has lost a lot of energy. He'll recharge, but it will take time."

"That means Juliette is out here? Right now?"

"Maybe."

"Jesus Christ!"

"Who?"

"Don't worry about it. I have to get back inside Mon Ciel right now."

Thunder exploded right next to Madeline, knocking her to the ground.

Juliette turned around, smiling at the hologram of Ayana. "Too late, it seems."

Madeline stood up and felt waves of energy pulsing from Juliette, who was standing several feet away. She could feel the vibrations through her entire body. She understood what Tadgh had said— Juliette was not *just* a hologram.

Juliette glanced at Madeline. The air around Juliette started to stir. "Who will protect you now? Let these stupid Sciphils come. I'll crush all of you at once," Juliette said as she strode toward Madeline.

CHAPTER 11

Madeline ran to her car while Juliette laughed maniacally. She jumped into the car and turned the ignition, starting the car. Juliette stirred the air. It spun around in the same way it had at the cemetery. Madeline backed the car out.

"Coward!" Juliette laughed. Madeline floored the gas pedal and drove the car straight at Juliette. The wind wall had not yet built up strong enough to protect Juliette.

Madeline felt the hit. Juliette's body was pushed backward, rolling on the ground, distorted. Madeline backed the car up and charged again. The second hit almost ripped Juliette in half.

The distorted Juliette stood up, angry. She roared and tried to put her body back together.

Juliette created the wind circle again.

Madeline accelerated once more.

Juliette took a stance and swung her arm. The car lifted up and spun around as if made of paper. There was no wind circle this time. It was a direct hit with the air pressure coming forth from Juliette's arms.

Without her seatbelt on, Madeline rolled around inside the car like a rag doll. She had the sickening feeling that she had broken her neck and her limbs had fallen off and were scattered somewhere in the car.

The car slammed down next to the creek.

It was the creek where she had almost drowned with Stefan. Madeline heard the water running fast. She climbed out of the destroyed car.

Juliette stood on a small hill, a smirk on her face. She swung her arms again.

Madeline found herself spun up into the air, then thrown down and submersed in the cold water. The pressure kept Madeline under the water.

From beneath the flowing creek, Madeline could see the light. It was the sort of light people who were dying would see. It was like being tied down in a cave in the dark, and looking up and seeing a faint spot of light, a spot of life, but knowing she would never get to it. The light became dimmer. And dimmer. And then it was completely black.

All of a sudden, the pressure lifted.

A basic survival instinct told Madeline to push up. She gasped for air at the surface and coughed up a mouthful of water. She got herself to the bank of the creek and slowly staggered to dry land.

On the hill in front of her, Richard and Ayana were fighting Juliette. Although there were two of them against one, it did not look as if they were winning.

Richard took a hit and fell. Ayana stopped Juliette from using that advantage to kill Richard, taking a hit herself.

She could run back to Mon Ciel like a coward right now, Madeline thought.

Hell!

Madeline dragged herself up the hill to where her grandfather and Ayana were fighting Juliette.

She approached the light circle, but she hit an invisible wall—the same kind of wall that had locked her out in the hologame when Ciaran was fighting with Juliette.

She couldn't penetrate it. She grabbed a fallen tree branch and hit it, but the branch bounced back, further numbing her already numb arms, body, and mind. She stood hopeless and helpless, watching her grandfather and Ayana being beaten mercilessly by Juliette.

The shadow of someone walked past her.

It might not have been a shadow, but a person walking at an incredible speed.

A man penetrated the invisible wall and charged at Juliette with a burning orange sword.

This was not a typical sword fight. They were testing the strength of their energy. The swords were just outlets. Each swing of the swords created a wave of wind and electrical currents. Juliette stumbled and staggered when the man with the orange sword attacked her. But she regained her position quickly.

She advanced and slashed at the man with the orange sword. His blood dripped on the ground. It looked like she was too powerful for him.

Judging by the wind that blew around their faces, the force of the foreign objects that flew around them, and the damage caused by each blow of the swords, Madeline knew there had to be an incredible amount of energy being exchanged within the world surrounded by the invisible wall.

"Please don't, Juliette. You don't have to kill everyone," Ayana said.

Juliette turned to Ayana and snarled, " He attacked me first. He deserves to die. All of you do. All of those who are against me deserve to die."

Juliette walked toward Ayana. "Especially you."

Madeline was so sure that Juliette would kill Ayana this time. But the man with the orange sword pulled out a dagger and lunged at Juliette.

Juliette whirled around with incredible speed. Her claws were out, ready for a sure kill. She could already taste the blood of her prey.

A ray of the morning's first sunlight ran across the ground. It was the most beautiful sunlight Madeline had ever seen.

In her rage, Juliette had neglected to notice the approaching rays. The light brushed against her holographic figure and sent her into flames. She hissed in pain and vanished quickly into thin air.

"Saved by the sunlight! How cinematic!" Madeline mumbled.

Although wounded, Ayana's composure did not waver. She glanced at Madeline. "Attacking Juliette head on! You're a brave woman, Madeline. The sunlight weakens Juliette, but it won't kill her. Wind is her strength, and sunlight is her weakness."

Madeline wanted to ask what would kill Juliette. But the world around her started to fade.

Richard managed to stand up.

Ayana glanced at the man with the orange sword. "What took you so long to get here?"

"You sent me to rescue four subjects on two different continents, Ayana. I am on Earth. I have to take some of their physical rules into account."

Ayana cast a warm look at him. "Thank you. I know we can rely on you. How was the subject in Australia?"

"He's strong. He actually saved himself. Good choice of a successor, Ayana."

Ayana's face brightened with a gracious smile. "Thank you Sciphil Nine. You will have a good one yourself one day."

Sciphil Nine nodded and smiled.

Richard approached Madeline. She felt as if her body had transcended beyond suffering. She was numb and not at all sure she was still conscious. Yet she must be because she could hear them talking. But Richard said something, and she had no idea what he meant by it.

She was drunk with her pain.

Sciphil Nine walked through the invisible wall again. Ayana smiled at him from the other side.

He approached Madeline. "I'll take you back to Mon Ciel."

"I owe you one, Sciphil Nine. I know Zach isn't an easy character to work with. If there is anything you need from me in the future, you need only ask," Ayana told him from inside the light circle.

Sciphil Nine looked at Ayana. "You're wrong, Ayana. Zach Flynn is not only easy to work with—he could make quite a spectacular Sciphil. I'm jealous, to be honest."

"Who did you say is her successor?" Madeline asked.

"Zach Flynn from Australia. Do you know him?"

Madeline gave Sciphil Nine a blank look and then fainted into his arms.

CHAPTER 12

The sun rose high over the hill, casting a warm glow over the rolling hills and meadows. It was one of those rare days in the English winter where the sky was blue and clear.

Unfortunately, the stunning weather did nothing to soothe Ciaran's mood as he walked down the long drive, approaching a tall man standing in front of Mon Ciel's gate. The man carried Madeline in his arms.

In the darkest corner of Ciaran's mind, he wanted what his father had warned him against for so many years: destruction.

He thirsted for blood.

His need to destroy was as tenacious as his passion to create. Throughout his whole life, he had strived to maintain a balance between destruction and creation. That balance was off kilter now, tilted toward the negative.

He knew Tadgh and Jo trailed behind him despite the fact he had asked them to stay in the house. Tadgh would never let him go outside Mon Ciel by himself, and Jo had been worried sick about Madeline since early in the morning.

Ciaran adjusted his coat quickly, checking to see that his gun was still in place. It was.

Based on the proximity of the gate and the man's location, Ciaran speculated that he was one of those Sciphils who could not penetrate Mon Ciel's protective shield. The man appeared tall and strong. He carried Madeline as if she was a sleeping doll.

Ciaran was sure she was injured. But if so, the damage had been done. Sheer willpower could play no role in fixing this. She had fooled him—and fooled herself—in order to go out there, and that had caused her harm.

As they got closer, Tadgh said, "I recognize him. He helped us when Juliette attacked us at Mrs. Hanson's. I think he's friendly, Ciaran," Tadgh said.

Ciaran didn't respond. He trusted no one. Especially now.

"Stay here," Ciaran brusquely directed as he approached the edge of the gate. Jo and Tadgh followed. Ciaran turned around.

"Stay here." His repeat was more like a growl.

Tadgh and Jo stayed back.

Ciaran sauntered past the gate of Mon Ciel.

The man observed Ciaran's every move. "You're confident, Ciaran."

"And you are?"

"I'm Pete Chandler, Sciphil Nine of Eudaiz."

Ciaran nodded. "Mr. Chandler, I'd like Madeline to be taken inside. I understand you cannot come inside Mon Ciel. I'll stay out here and discuss whatever you want."

Sciphil Nine laughed. "You're a businessman, or so I was told. On top of all the other qualities that set you up as a great ruler."

"I'm not a ruler of any kind. Madeline needs to be tended to. Please let my brother take her inside. Then we can talk."

Sciphil Nine nodded.

Trusting, Ciaran thought. He could easily take Madeline inside and break his promise to this man. Ciaran approached Sciphil Nine. The energy coming from Pete Chandler was very different from the kind that had emanated from Ayana. By Ciaran's gauge, Pete Chandler was human, with a body made of flesh and blood.

That meant Ciaran could put a bullet through the body and end all negotiations.

Ciaran took Madeline gently from Sciphil Nine and walked back inside Mon Ciel to where Tadgh and Jo were waiting.

"Doctor Thomas," Ciaran said.

"Already called," Tadgh responded.

A helicopter arrived, hovered in the air, and touched down on the helicopter landing pad in the adjacent garden. Doctor Thomas climbed out and made a beeline toward Tadgh.

After a quick visual examination, he said, "Let's get her inside."

"Thank you for coming quickly, Doctor," Ciaran said.

Tadgh and Jo scurried toward the house.

"You're not coming?"

Ciaran nodded toward the gate. "Soon. But I have something to see to first."

Doctor Thomas nodded. Before he turned away, his eyes caught sight of Sciphil Nine and held for a moment. Then he rushed toward the house. Ciaran had caught the odd gaze from the doctor, but he said nothing.

Ciaran approached the gate but held back from stepping outside the grounds. He stood there with his hands in his pockets and observed Pete Chandler.

"You are human, Mr. Chandler?"

Pete nodded. "I have to go now. In fact, I should not be here at all. But I wanted to meet the man I would one day serve."

Ciaran exited the gate and approached Pete Chandler.

"How many Sciphils are there?" he asked.

"Nine."

"So you are the youngest?"

"The number indicates the order of arrival of the very first Sciphils to Alphi more than five hundred years ago. There have been several generations of successors down the line. The order is no longer applicable."

Ciaran nodded. "Who am I the successor of?"

"Sciphil Three."

"If I am his successor, why isn't he meeting with me?"

Pete smiled.

Ciaran nodded. "I understand. You can't tell me. Since you helped Madeline, what can I do for you?"

"Stay alive. Juliette broke the seal. She is no longer a Sciphil. But she has grown so strong. None of us can stop her."

"She was a Sciphil?"

Pete nodded. The steel wristband Pete was wearing flashed red. He glanced at it. "I have to go now. You can kill Juliette. You are the only one who can at the moment."

"I can't kill her twice," Ciaran snarled.

"But she's willing to kill you many times. She's no longer the Juliette you remember."

"Of course not—she a simulated electronic profile."

Pete shook his head. "She was brought to Eudaiz soon enough after she died on Earth. Her life force was still there, and it operates her profile. Look, it's not my place to say—"

"Then whose place is it?" Ciaran raised his voice.

"Yours."

"Bullshit."

"You have to come to terms with this, Ciaran. And the sooner, the better."

Ciaran pulled his gun and pointed it at Pete. "How about I come to terms right now?"

Pete smiled. "Your earthly weapon could kill every human, including you, but it will have no effect on me, Ciaran."

"And you expect me to kill the recreated Juliette using this weapon?"

"No. She has to be terminated properly. In Eudaiz."

"He will go to Eudaiz to be with me, not to kill me." Juliette's voice echoed in the air, and before Pete could react, his body was spun up high and smashed down to the ground.

Juliette stood in the shade of a resting station in the park, quite a distance away.

"Get back inside," Pete yelled and stood up.

A burst of air blew in Ciaran's direction. He could feel the vibration of energy coming from it. Pete charged at the air funnel and swung his sword. He sliced through the air before the funnel hit Ciaran, but the residual force threw Pete up again and pushed Ciaran backward. He fell and rolled on the ground.

Ciaran darted toward Pete to help him up. His hands were nearly burned when he touched Pete. Ciaran withdrew his hands.

"I'm using my Sciphil energy. You can't touch me."

"But you held Madeline before."

"I turned it off. I was a human when I held her."

"Then turn it off, and I'll take you inside Mon Ciel."

Pete shook his head. "Too risky. I've got to run now."

Another wedge of air struck at the grass near them, blasting a large hole in the ground. It was such a long distance, though, that Juliette had missed her true targets.

Pete stood up. "The sunlight has a vibration frequency that clashes with Juliette's energy sources. She will try to stay in the shade."

Another wedge of air slashed right in front of Ciaran, pushing him and causing him to fall again.

"Get inside and stay alive." It was Pete's voice that echoed back to him. The man had vanished into another dimension. Ciaran charged toward Mon Ciel's gate before another blow could come from Juliette.

CHAPTER 13

Madeline awoke and saw Ciaran working on a computer in the corner of his bedroom. She tried not to move. She liked to watch him work. His concentration was extreme. His intense eyes looked as if they could punch holes in the computer screen and set it on fire.

The more important reason for her not to move was that she needed to bide some time. She wasn't sure exactly how to break it to him that she couldn't be with him when he took his position as successor.

For both of them to stay alive, they couldn't be together.

She was unsure about many things in her life. But she knew what she had done in Australia ten years ago. And one thing she was certain of—her soul was no way virtuous.

She didn't have to move. He sensed her like a cat. He stopped working and strode to the bed. He smiled and checked the temperature of her forehead. Satisfied with what he felt, he asked, "How are you feeling?"

"I'm fine. How long have I been in bed?"

"Three hours."

Ciaran walked to the side table and grabbed the medicine and a glass of water. Doctor Thomas had examined her and had left clear instructions for Ciaran. Ciaran looked at the doctor's notes, checking them over. Then he brought the medicine over to the bed. His movements were meticulously efficient.

Madeline sat up, took the pills and the water. She downed the pills and gave Ciaran back the water.

His face was unfathomable. Inexplicably controlled. He stood holding the glass of water, looking at her, saying nothing.

"What's the damage?" she asked.

"You should be fine now. If you want to know the exact condition you were in, you'll have to ask Doctor Thomas."

That was cold! Madeline thought.

He knew exactly what condition she was in. He must be pissed that she had drugged him, putting him out of action the night before. If he wanted to play this passive-aggressive game, she could play.

"Could you pass me the phone, please? I'll give Doctor Thomas a call."

Ciaran nodded. He turned as if he was going to fetch her the phone. But instead, he heaved the glass to the wall. The glass shattered into pieces, and broken glass rained onto the floor.

Then he strode out of the room and slammed the door.

Jo immediately came into the room as if she had been waiting right outside.

Madeline waved her arms in the air. "He's pissed because I drugged him last night."

Jo said nothing. She sat on the bed and examined Madeline's bruised face. "Do you really think he's mad because of that?"

She looked into Jo's green eyes, eyes that were waiting for her honest answers. She couldn't hold it in any longer. The emotion stormed out of her like a tidal wave. Madeline wept.

Jo held her patiently and waited until her crying subsided. "I can't tell you what I felt when they brought you in because, on the rage chart, I was right at the bottom. When Ciaran finished talking to the man outside the gate—"

"Outside?"

"Yes, he had to go outside to get you."

Madeline nodded again.

"Doctor Thomas said the fact that you didn't die was pure luck. He substantiated the statement with an extensive report, of course. But to give Ciaran the lowdown, Doctor Thomas said that if your rib had been cracked an inch higher, or if you had been held under the water for a couple of seconds longer, there would have been nothing he could have done. So yes, you're fine now. But it was only because of dumb luck."

Madeline stared at Jo. Jo's eyes were full of resentment now. And that was what Jo described as 'the bottom of the rage chart'. What could Ciaran possibly be feeling? Like he'd been kicked in the teeth? Stabbed in the heart?

Madeline remembered when Ciaran had been shot at Fountains Abbey. The feeling of her boiling blood was still fresh in her mind. Still, Ciaran hadn't been the cause of his almost fatal injury. He hadn't stuck his chest out and dared Stefan to shoot at him.

And he had survived. He'd left the past behind to be with her. After all they had been through together . . . Now, she had to tell him that they couldn't be together anymore!

"Jo, I killed those people in the woods. It wasn't Zach's fault. It wasn't your fault. I had to kill them." Tears streamed down her face uncontrollably. "My soul is not virtuous. I can't be a successor. I can't be with Ciaran."

"He doesn't have to be a successor. He doesn't have to be with those Sciphils." Jo wiped the tears from Madeline's face.

She shook her head. "At the cemetery, Juliette forced Ayana to put a seal on Ciaran's successor position. If he doesn't take the position, he will die. If he knows I can't go with him, he'll try to get out of the deal."

"You can't be so sure, Madeline. And what if he can't get out of the deal?"

"He'll try. Please don't tell him, Jo. He *will* attempt to get out of the deal, and he will fail. I can feel it. Can you promise not to tell him? Please?"

Jo nodded, tears gleaming in her eyes.

"I'm going to be sick," she said to Jo.

Jo helped Madeline out of bed. They stumbled a few steps before Madeline slumped to the floor, violently ill.

Ciaran stormed into the room so fast that Jo doubted he had ever left. He tried to get to Madeline.

She pushed him away. She backed away from him on the floor. "Don't touch me. Don't touch. I'm dirty."

"Madeline."

"Leave me." Tears poured down her face now. "I made a mess. I'll clean it up."

"Darling. That's okay." Ciaran approached.

"Don't. Don't come near me. I'm a mess."

Ciaran scooped Madeline off the floor and carried her to the bed. He cradled her while she wept into his chest. Then she looked at Jo and saw a spark of anger in her eyes before she turned on her heel and stormed out of the room.

CHAPTER 14

TJ stood at the end of the back corridor connecting to the old kitchen, lips pulled back, revealing his sharp little teeth. Regardless of how formidable and intimidating full-grown Alaskan Malamutes could look, TJ was still a puppy.

The more petulantly he behaved, the more puppyish he would appear to the thirteen-year-old cat Migi. The cat sat across the corridor, looking bored with TJ's show of ferocity. She cast a dismissive glance at him, then she lowered herself down to the floor and started washing herself.

Tadgh frowned. He felt pity for the puppy but decided not to help. He had to learn for himself to be a proper grown-up dog one day.

From the other end of the corridor, Jo stomped right past Tadgh and the animals. If he wasn't mistaken, he saw tears in her eyes. She had just come from Ciaran's room. *What could it be?* Tadgh wondered.

"What do you think?" he asked Migi.

The cat that had been mutilated by Mrs. Hanson was the most wicked of all the animals Tadgh had known. She had saved him from Juliette once. Migi wagged her twin tails, pointing the tips of her tails toward different directions. Tadgh nodded, "Conflicting emotions. Must have something to do with Madeline."

Then he frowned. Jo was heading toward the back gardens. He shot up and darted after her. When he caught up with her, she had almost reached the back door.

"Where do you think you're going?"

"Out, isn't it obvious?"

"But Juliette is out there . . ."

"That's why I'm going. I'm going to teach the bitch a lesson." Jo approached the door.

"That's a man's job."

Jo turned around. "And that comment will earn you a slap in the face."

"Then come back in here and do it. I promise I won't duck!"

Jo glared at Tadgh and continued to the back gardens.

"Fuck this!" Tadgh mumbled and darted after her.

Outside the gate, the field opened onto rolling green hills. Jo stood, looking out into the far distance. Tadgh came up behind her. "For pity's sake, Jo. Please come back inside the house."

"I've decided that I'm taking Madeline back to New York tomorrow. I just wanted to enjoy a bit of the countryside before we left."

Tadgh shrugged. "All right. But we can talk about this inside."

"I have an experiment to carry out here. You go inside. I can't cover you."

"You? Cover me? With your five foot body, including those sticks you are standing on."

"Five foot *two*."

"Well, those two inches certainly make a huge difference."

"Those precious two inches make a difference to *me*. Get out of my sight, Tadgh. I'm busy here."

"Are you looking for me?" It was Juliette's voice, wafting on the thin air.

"Fuck me." Tadgh snatched Jo and pushed her behind him. They both looked around but saw no sign of Juliette. The rolling green hills were covered in sunlight just as before.

"Do you think you can stand in the sun and be safe from me?" Juliette said sarcastically.

Tadgh looked around. He could not see her.

"In there." Jo nodded toward a small resting station just a bit further up the hill.

"How do you know?"

Before Jo could answer, the door of the resting station swung open. Juliette stood inside, a wind circle already spinning. Its span enlarged, but it could not reach Jo and Tadgh. The most damage it did was chopping at the nearby grass.

Jo pushed Tadgh aside. A smile came over her foxy face. "It's my turn now."

She pulled her tiny travel makeup box from her bag and flicked the lid open. Inside were square compartments of eye shadow, lipstick, blush, and a mirror that occupied the entire half of the lid. She tilted the mirror and caught the sunlight, so it reflected straight onto Juliette.

Juliette screamed as if she had been shot.

"Again!" Jo commanded herself. She reflected one more time. Juliette staggered. A hole burned through the middle of her image. The wind circle vanished.

Tadgh was flabbergasted.

Juliette was furious. Her voice rumbled like thunder. "Don't you dare try that trick on me!"

"It's not a trick. It's a lethal weapon. You're doomed, you sadistic bitch." Jo grinned. "You can beam away now."

Juliette hid in a corner of the station where Jo could not reflect the sunlight. She refused to beam away.

A hovering cloud dragged a shadow closer behind Jo and Tadgh. Tadgh turned around and saw it.

"Shit," Tadgh said. He pulled at Jo.

Jo turned around and immediately registered the danger.

They raced toward the gate.

They moved as fast as they could.

The cloud created a shadow right against Mon Ciel's fence, and Juliette beamed right into the shadow. She stood blocking Tadgh's and Jo's way back inside Mon Ciel.

"You're right. I derive pleasure from other people's pain." She swung her arms, and a blast of freezing air flew at them. Tadgh plucked Jo up and swiveled aside. The blade of air dug into the ground nearby, blew up a large hole, and funneled dirt, grass, and rocks up into the sky.

A piece of rock hit Tadgh in the head. He fell on top of Jo.

From inside the backyard, the puppy TJ and Migi charged out, running straight at Juliette from behind. They knocked her out of the shadow, and the contact with the sunlight burned her again. Juliette hissed, roared, and beamed away.

Tadgh was too dazed to move himself in the right direction. Jo pulled him with her into the backyard. Once there, Tadgh flopped down onto the grass.

"Look at me, Tadgh. How many fingers?"

She held two fingers in front of him. Tadgh blinked. "Five foot two inches."

Jo rubbed her hand on Tadgh's head. "It's a pretty big lump. You're going to have a huge headache."

"Could you check on TJ and Migi?"

"What?"

"See if they're okay," Tadgh mumbled, his voice slurred with a concussion.

Before Jo made a move, Migi strode into the garden, grabbing TJ by the crook of his neck. She dropped the dog down onto the grass. There was a gash on TJ's front leg. Migi licked the wound. The puppy snarled at first but then submitted to Migi's care.

Outside the garden, on the hillside, Juliette lingered in the shadow of a cloud whenever she found one.

"Look out, Juliette!" Jo muttered and helped Tadgh up. "Come on, let's get you inside."

CHAPTER 15

Dusk quickly blanketed the hillside in front of Mon Ciel. Ciaran stood at the entrance, ready to go. His long black coat billowed in the winter breeze. He shifted his left shoulder slightly, easing the tense muscles there caused by the number of injuries his shoulder had suffered. More importantly, he checked to see that his much-needed weapons were in place and ready to go.

It was time to settle any debts, resentment, and lingering hatred that remained in his life.

In the last few days, it had taken a lot of work. It had taken a tremendous amount of careful planning and preparation from everyone inside Mon Ciel. Now, it was time for Ciaran to execute the plan. It was time for him to regain control of his life and the lives of those he loved.

They were not going to be caged inside Mon Ciel.

He sauntered outside the gate. He paused and waited. He strolled a little further down the hill.

The rolling hills were quiet. There was not even the sound of an insect, a wild animal, or the wind blowing in the trees.

The air thickened.

A flash of blue light sliced through the air, and the hologram of Ayana Dee appeared.

"Ayana, there is nothing for you to do here."

Ayana smiled. "I'm pleased to see you decide to take action, Ciaran. But you are not equipped to fight Juliette. We aren't strong enough to protect you."

"I'll negotiate with her."

"She won't negotiate. She just wants you."

"At least she's clear about what she wants. You and the other Sciphils want me to be a Sciphil and serve a universe that I don't care at all about, at an unknown cost to my family."

"You misconstrue what we want . . ."

"That's the most logical conclusion I can draw from what you told me. Now, I will call Juliette to talk to her. I assume it's best for you to leave to avoid being hurt."

"Are you sure about this, Ciaran? You don't have to do this on your own."

"I will not fight with Juliette. Therefore, I don't need any help from you. Am I making myself clear?"

Ayana's intense blue eyes blinked with confusion and disappointment. She nodded, and her hologram disappeared. The air returned to its mysterious quietness.

"Juliette, I know you heard me. If you want to talk, now is the time."

Nothing happened. Ciaran waited for a moment.

"I thought you wanted me," he said and turned go back to Mon Ciel.

Then he felt it—a vibration of energy filling the air. Juliette's image glowed in the darkness. "Ciaran, I'm glad you've decided to come to me."

Ciaran observed her carefully. From a distance, he couldn't tell if Juliette was a hologram or an actual presence.

"I don't know how I can come to you."

"Via the Daimon Gate. I told you that already."

"And what exactly will it require of me?"

Juliette looked puzzled. No response.

Ciaran deduced that if Juliette was merely an electronic profile—due to her human life ending years ago—then the fact that Ciaran was a successor would be unknown to her, and she would not have an answer for this question. The solution to this problem would not be available to her because it was not a part of the data input she had received.

Artificial intelligence and robotic behavior were child's play to Ciaran.

"I'm a human, and I'm alive, Juliette. Whatever the Daimon Gate is, do you honestly think I can pass through it and still be with you? Are you alive or are you not?"

Juliette again looked perplexed.

"Daimon Gate is a nine-level transmutation process, categorized in three stages, where biological and psychological profiles are purified. If an individual is proven to be worthy, he or she will pass the gate and become a perfect entity. If an individual is not worthy, he or she will not reform, and will thus be exterminated during the process."

That was definitely a robotic pre-programmed answer, Ciaran mused. He stepped closer to Juliette.

"Do you think I am worthy? What if I die during the process? Can I still be with you? Or do I have to die to be with you?"

Juliette appeared to be even more confused.

"I died on Earth."

"Yes, you did. But your body was not placed in the coffin. How did you get to Alphi?"

"I am not in Alphi. I am in Eudaiz. The Daimon Gate will lead you to Eudaiz."

"But only if I pass the test. What if I fail? I'll die. How can I be with you then?"

Juliette's face started to turn red. Ciaran had befuddled the machine. He stepped closer and reached out for her. He could feel the energy, the vibration. There was the presence of solid substance. Like Tadgh said, this was not a hologram.

"Do you want to be with me or not?" Ciaran asked.

His hand touched Juliette's arm. It was solid, and it didn't burn him. Juliette looked up at Ciaran. "Yes, I do. I want to be with you."

"Where is the Daimon Gate?"

"It depends on the astronomical time and location. All dimensions have to be open on Earth and connected."

"How many dimensions?"

"Nine"

"That's manageable. Science has gotten it to eleven dimensions."

Juliette smiled. "Times nine."

"Oh, for pity's sake, Juliette. I can't manage that."

"Yes, you can. Run the disk."

"If I find the gate, so what? You're speaking about some kind of wormhole. This is science fiction to those like myself who are still alive and living on Earth."

"It's not as primitive as a wormhole, Ciaran . . ."

Ciaran shook his head. "I have a proposal. Why don't you come to me? Like now. You're here. Why don't you just stay here? We can be together this way, can't we?"

Ciaran grabbed Juliette. Her body was solid. Not solid like flesh and bones, but much more than frequencies and signals.

Juliette trembled as if she wanted to agree with Ciaran.

"I can't stay."

"Why not?" Ciaran held Juliette now. Her image glowed in his arms.

"I don't know. I can't stay. You have to come to me. You have to be with me. There is no other way."

Juliette's body started to vibrate. She reached her arms up and held onto Ciaran. But all he felt was a ring of bone-crushing force wrapped around him. He grunted out in pain and slumped to the ground.

Juliette released him. She reached out again to help him up, but Ciaran gestured for her to keep her distance.

"You're going to kill me now if you touch me."

Juliette stopped.

Ciaran stood up. "Juliette, I want to be with you. But I don't want to die. You don't really want to kill me, do you?"

Silence.

"The Daimon Gate will kill me in much the same way as you touching me now. No matter what the transmutational process is within the gate, I'll die. I'm sure that I'm not a worthy individual. I'm a human being with a corrupted soul. If you once loved me, you'd know that about me."

Ciaran started to walk back to Mon Ciel. Juliette followed but kept at a distance.

"If you want, you can stick around. I can see you at night. Just like this. We can talk, keeping a distance. What do you think?"

This was obviously not something Juliette had in her program. It was not something she had considered.

They approached the gate. Juliette stopped at a distance from it.

"I'm going in now. Good night, Juliette."

"No, this is not going to work."

"Then give me a plausible solution." Ciaran had to raise his voice so Juliette could hear since she was quite far away.

"You go through the Daimon Gate and be with me properly."

Ciaran stood close to the fence so that he could easily dive inside Mon Ciel's boundaries.

"If I promise you that I'll go through the Daimon Gate, will you let me leave now?"

Juliette smiled. "No."

"I thought not. I guess you want to take me, dump me right in front of the Daimon Gate, and make me go through it, regardless of whether I could see it or not."

Juliette grinned. "You know me too well, Ciaran. As I said, I'll have you, either dead or alive. If I let you leave now, I'll never have you again."

"I wish we could find a better solution," Ciaran said softly so that Juliette had to move closer to hear. I remember every day we were together. Those were happy days."

"Speak up."

"I know what you have on the disk."

"I said speak up!" Juliette moved closer.

Forty more feet, Ciaran thought. He needed Juliette to move forty feet closer. Ciaran left the gate and walked about ten feet toward her. He stood there, his hands jammed in his pockets.

"What do you want me to do, Juliette?"

"Speak up." She moved ten feet closer. "What are you saying?" she asked.

Ciaran shrugged. He looked at Juliette. The look that had always softened her heart . . . and for how many years? She advanced another ten feet and stood still.

Ciaran turned around and strolled toward Mon Ciel again.

Juliette galloped forward another ten feet. Then she stopped again. Ciaran felt a wedge of wind hit his back with force. The wind lifted him up and threw him fifty feet from Mon Ciel's gate. Ciaran both heard and felt his bones rattle. He stood up.

Juliette wore an evil smirk on her face. Her loving expression had been replaced with fury. Her eyes were on fire. *There is no other solution*, Ciaran thought. He stood up straight, and as he did, he pulled two guns from his back waistband.

These were no ordinary weapons—they were two specialized laser guns that simulated the profile of sunlight, an idea inspired by Jo's little experiment with her makeup mirror in the back garden.

He shot at Juliette. Each beam sent her staggering back several feet toward Mon Ciel. Each beam punched a burning hole in her body. She squealed, hissed, screamed, and staggered back with every shot.

Ciaran kept shooting, pushing her back. Ten feet more would do the trick, he thought.

Juliette whirled around, trying to regain her balance. Her brain was frantically trying to register new information and process it for alternative solutions. She hissed and screamed then suddenly stood up straight. The burning holes in her body started to heal. The wind circle around her started to stir.

She laughed.

Ciaran continued to shoot. His two beams barely made a scratch on her body now. She had somehow established a defense mechanism against the sun's rays.

The wind circle grew sharp, cutting into the grass like the blades of a hedge trimmer. Ciaran kept attacking with the two guns, but they seemed to have no effect. He strode toward her to avoid her approaching him and veered away from Mon Ciel.

Behind Mon Ciel's fence, Tadgh, Jo, and Madeline darted out with two guns each.

"Yo!" Tadgh called out.

Juliette turned around, looking at Tadgh. She approached Tadgh, Jo, and Madeline, inadvertently moving closer to Mon Ciel.

They shot. Six beams at a time created an impact. Juliette staggered. The holes in her body took a little longer to heal this time. But they did heal.

Tadgh, Jo, and Madeline kept shooting.

Juliette smiled. She swung her arms to create a deadly wedge of wind that she flung at them at head height. It almost decapitated them. They ducked, crawling on the ground.

Juliette laughed and prepared for a second swipe.

Behind her, a beam exploded from a device Ciaran held. It blew Juliette five feet further toward Mon Ciel. Her back was on fire. She whirled around several times to put it out. She screamed in rage.

Ciaran added his two guns attack and charged toward Juliette.

He knew that as soon as she put out the fire, they would be back to square one.

When Ciaran got to Juliette, the fire had just gone out. But she had not yet had time to create another blast of wind.

Ciaran dove at her, trying to tackle her backward.

She grabbed him, and he felt his bones breaking in her grip. He kept pushing. Five feet wasn't much. His body could hold until then. Two more seconds, he promised himself. He closed his eyes and kept pushing.

Juliette snarled and tried to shove Ciaran away from her.

One second.

There. In position.

Ciaran shouted out his command. "Fire!"

CHAPTER 16

Two towers of light from inside Mon Ciel's fence beamed out a fifty-foot cone of simulated sunlight. It was the equivalent of two thousand single beams of sunlight.

It was too fast. It was too strong.

Juliette screamed a blood-curdling scream and exploded into nothingness.

Ciaran sat on his heels, staring at the space where Juliette had disintegrated. He wasn't sure what he felt. He was probably too numb to feel anything.

Ciaran staggered up. Madeline approached. She squeezed his arms. "Let's go inside."

Ciaran nodded. He rubbed his thumb along the dimple on her left cheek and kissed her before they headed back toward the house.

In the Great Reception room, Ciaran settled in a chair next to Madeline. The painkillers had taken effect. His bodily pain was lost in a fog now.

Jo shared a couch with Migi in a corner of the room.

Next to the side table and an elegant lamp, George LeBlanc, Ciaran and Tadgh's cousin from France, sat in a comfortable reading chair.

George was in his early forties although he looked much younger than his age. Brown hair framed his intelligent face and brightened his sharp, gray eyes.

The gray eyes were a shared feature in the LeBlanc family, Madeline thought. But while Ciaran's gray was deep, smoky, and intense, Tadgh's was witty, and George's was soft and kind.

Tadgh walked into the room with a bottle in his hand. "Found it. This should suit everyone. It's very delicate."

Coming from the LeBlanc's cellar, Madeline was assured of its delicacy and was sure it would suit everyone's taste.

Tadgh served everyone.

"How's the pain?" Madeline asked Ciaran.

He smiled. "Gone!" he exclaimed.

"Doctor Thomas is staying here overnight in case we need him."

Ciaran shook his head. "He needs a family to go home to. Where is he now?"

"In the guest room. Reading, I think."

Ciaran and Madeline took their glasses of wine from Tadgh.

"He's never had a family?" Madeline asked.

Ciaran shook his head. "He did. I don't know what happened to them, though. Doctor Thomas is a very private man. I don't think it's appropriate to ask about his personal affairs if he's not willing to share."

"A private man working for the LeBlancs?" Madeline exaggerated the statement by rolling her eyes. Ciaran laughed and kissed her cheek.

"Thank you for your help, George, especially on such short notice," Ciaran addressed his cousin.

"You put on a good show. I enjoyed it. I'm glad my expertise was of some use." George grinned.

Madeline had just discovered another resemblance in the LeBlancs—their gorgeous grins.

Ciaran said to Jo and Madeline, "Sorry I didn't have enough time to explain to you in the last few days. George is the top man in show business in

Paris. Stringing a few light bulbs together wasn't a problem for him, as you have seen."

"I've got to give it to you, George. It was brilliant. Especially since we didn't have a chance for a test run and had no room for error." Tadgh raised his wine in salute.

George shook his head. "I just pushed a button . . . I can't believe Juliette ended up like that. I still don't understand . . ."

"No need for you to dig in further, George," Ciaran cut in. "I appreciate your help. We should close this chapter and consider it done."

George shrugged. "All right. Up to you. We're family. I don't mind helping. Don't be too harsh on the people around you. And realize that you don't have to be perfect. You don't have to take care of everything."

"I beg your pardon." Ciaran lowered his voice.

"Come on! This is a time to celebrate," Tadgh reminded him.

"Yes, we worked hard for this victory," Jo agreed.

Madeline looked at Ciaran. His eyes looked tired as if he were drunk. But he had hardly touched his wine.

"Are you okay?" she asked him.

"I think my head is going to roll right off my shoulders."

"I'll take you to bed."

Ciaran nodded. "Please excuse me, everyone. Apparently those hits were harder than I thought." Ciaran stood up and walked out of the room with Madeline scurrying after him.

In the hallway, Ciaran staggered. He leaned against the wall. Madeline wrapped her arm around his waist for support, and they walked toward the bedroom.

In front of the door to the bedroom, they found Doctor Thomas waiting.

"Doctor, what can I do for you?"

"Are you okay, Ciaran?"

"Painkillers and wine have turned out to be a poor mix. Come on in."

Ciaran pushed the bedroom door open and staggered inside. He slumped into the reading chair.

"What would you like to talk about, Doctor Thomas? Is it about the man you saw in front of Mon Ciel a few days ago? The one who carried Madeline home from the creek?"

Doctor Thomas smiled. "You don't miss a thing, do you, Ciaran? Yes, I'm here about that man. I've seen him before. He's been inside Mon Ciel, talking to your mother. That was before you were born. Your parents had just moved into this place. I don't know if this information is significant at all, but I thought I should tell you."

"Thanks, Doctor Thomas. That's a very important piece of information."

Ciaran stood up and moved clumsily toward the bed and climbed in. "I'm sorry. I've never been this drunk before . . ." His words trailed off, and he flopped down onto the pillows.

Madeline darted toward the bed. Feeling his forehead, she said, "Jesus Christ, Doctor, I don't think he's drunk. He's burning up."

Doctor Thomas took Ciaran's pulse and then rushed out of the room to get his medical bag.

Ciaran no longer responded to Madeline's voice. Juliette had something to do with this. Madeline knew it. She knew Juliette couldn't be killed so easily. Going to the intercom, she called to the Great Reception room.

Tadgh, Jo, and George arrived at the same time as the doctor.

While Doctor Thomas examined Ciaran, Madeline paced back and forth at the end of the bed. "It has to have something to do with Juliette. I knew it wouldn't be that easy to kill her."

Doctor Thomas finished his examination.

That was way too quick, Madeline thought.

Everyone looked at the doctor, waiting for his diagnosis. "This has nothing to do with his injuries or what just happened," he told them. "Ciaran is experiencing something similar to what happened to you when you inhaled that potion, Madeline. Your body was comatose."

"But we didn't see him inhale anything. We drank the same wine, ate the same food tonight," Tadgh said.

"Comatose. Doctor, you are saying that there is nothing you can do? That he has to wake up by himself? Are you sure this is the same condition I had?"

Doctor Thomas nodded. "Unfortunately yes."

Madeline remembered her experience vividly. She remembered how she drifted away and was desperate for Ciaran to do something to pull her back. She would not let that happen to him.

Madeline leaped onto the bed and shook his shoulders.

"Ciaran, stay with me. Answer me. Give me a sign. Please!"

She remembered the cold and dark place, the chapel where Juliette pulled her in and then burned her. Madeline shook Ciaran's shoulders again and again. "Please don't go there. Please, Ciaran. Answer me."

Madeline shook him so violently she was afraid she might break his neck. But there was no response from Ciaran.

Jo approached Madeline. "No, Jo. I know what I'm doing."

Madeline shook him again. This time, he responded. He muttered something unintelligible.

"What are you saying, Ciaran?" Madeline asked.

He said something again, very softly.

"It's in French." Madeline looked at the others. She didn't realize she was weeping. "It's French," she repeated.

Tadgh and George moved toward the bed.

Ciaran mumbled the French words again.

"He said if they release his mother, he'll do anything."

Ciaran's body tensed, then it went lax. He said nothing more. Madeline knew he had gone to the dark place where she had been. She had to do something better than watching and waiting. She had to talk to her grandfather.

Madeline hopped off the bed. "I need to talk to my grandfather outside Mon Ciel. Would you go with me, Tadgh?"

"You have to ask?"

"I'll go, too," Jo said.

"Please stay and look after Ciaran. I need you here."

Jo nodded. "Okay."

Madeline and Tadgh rushed out of the room.

CHAPTER 17

Madeline and Tadgh ran in the dark. They charged through Mon Ciel's gate.

"Grandfather!" Madeline called out.

Nothing happened.

"Ayana Dee!" Tadgh called.

Still nothing.

"Sciphil Nine! Pete Chandler! Anyone, for fuck's sake!" Tadgh yelled.

The air thickened. The hologram of Richard Kelley appeared, his eyes bleary and his hair a mess.

"We're a little preoccupied because of what you just did. Stop yelling, Tadgh," Richard directed.

"Shouldn't you be thanking us for killing Juliette?" Tadgh said.

"Grandfather, we didn't kill her, did we? Is she taking Ciaran now?"

"Madeline, you killed her presence."

"What does that mean, exactly?" Tadgh asked.

Richard wiped at his sweating forehead. "As a Sciphil, she won't die like a human being. The only way to end her existence is to terminate her energy source at her tower. I can't access her tower."

"We killed her presence. Does that mean we're halfway to killing her completely?" Madeline asked.

Richard shook his head. "What you did was incapacitate her temporarily. You pushed her back to her tower. There, she will use her eudqi to form another presence. Once she forms again, she will be invincible."

"Eudqi? Do I need a new dictionary?" Tadgh asked.

"A eudqi is a life force made of multiple astrological sources of energy. We have nine Sciphils, and eight of them hold major sources of eudqi. The king is a Sciphil who uses his own eudqi to combine the other eight and make it a unified eudqi that sustains Eudaiz. The king's eudqi is the strongest, and only he can terminate the other Sciphils. The other eight cannot terminate one another."

"Okay, so you can't disconnect Juliette from her eudqi, and now she will reform and be invincible. I guess blowing up her presence was a fucked-up plan. But it wasn't our fault. But how does taking Ciaran fix the problem?" Tadgh asked in frustration.

"What do you mean by Ciaran being taken?"

"He's comatose and negotiating in French for a release of our mother. Isn't that the condition you and Juliette created to get to Madeline before?" Tadgh asked.

"What we created was a hybrid hologame. In Eudaiz, only Juliette controls the games. But she is not in control of herself right now. So how can she be controlling Ciaran?"

"So who is doing this now?"

"I have a theory, but if I tell you, you have to do something for me afterward, Madeline."

"If anything happens to Ciaran, I won't follow through with anything I promised you before, let alone what I'm promising now."

"I don't have a choice, Madeline."

"Fine. Say it if you must. I'll see what I can do."

"The disk that Juliette created has a program that helps humans enter the Daimon Gate. It's at the villa outside London. You've been there. I need you to retrieve it. If you need to enter the Daimon Gate without me, use it."

"Is that all?"

Richard nodded.

"Okay, I'll do it. What's your theory about Ciaran's current condition?"

Richard contemplated. "Ciaran is the successor of Sciphil Three, the King of Eudaiz."

"Fuck me," Tadgh mumbled.

"Although the king is still in control of his eudqi, and his presence is still intact, no one has been able to contact him for more than thirty years."

"You've lost your king?" Tadgh shook his head.

"He's still in charge. He knows what is happening in Eudaiz. He just hasn't connected or taken any action. When Juliette reforms, it will be disastrous for Eudaiz. The only person who can terminate Juliette is the king. If you were the king, and for some reason, you could not take action yourself, what would you do?"

"I'd get my successor to do it," Madeline said.

"Exactly." Richard nodded.

"So let's get this clear . . . The current king wants Ciaran to go through the Daimon Gate—which sounds a lot like jumping through the gates of hell—to get to Eudaiz, become king, and kill Juliette, who at that point might have become invincible already. Piece of cake!" Tadgh retorted.

"I know it's not easy. That's why I think Ciaran is receiving some training now. The king cannot connect with us, but Ayana activated the seal of the successor on Ciaran's arm a few days ago, so the king might be able to connect with his successor now. But that's only a theory."

"You're saying Ciaran is in a hologame now?" Tadgh asked.

"The king built the first super artificial intelligence system in the multiverse. The system ran Eudaiz flawlessly while he was in absence for more than thirty years. If the training comes from him, it won't be just a hologame, Tadgh."

"What can we do to help him?" Madeline asked.

"If you have faith in God, then pray."

The hologram of Richard flickered and disappeared.

Madeline stormed into the bedroom. Tadgh followed. The room was as quiet as a tomb. Jo sat at the end of the bed, holding a damp cloth, confused and worried. Before Madeline could ask, Jo hopped off the bed and shoved the cloth into Madeline's hands.

"He's burning up like an oven. I can't watch this. Did you get any info? Is there anything I can do to feel less useless?"

Madeline pulled the sleeve of Ciaran's shirt up, revealing the crucifix tattoo glowing white and blue.

"Jesus Christ, Grandfather was right. The king must have Ciaran in some form of a game."

"A hologame?" Jo asked.

"He said it might be something more complicated and advanced than a hologame."

Ciaran grunted as if he had been hit. His body tensed up and convulsed like he was in a fight—or being beaten up. Madeline jumped on the bed. She held Ciaran's hands. As soon as he felt her hands on his, he gripped them.

"Ciaran, please come back to me!" Madeline cried out.

Ciaran squeezed Madeline's hands, and his body gradually loosened up.

Jo stared, contemplating. Then she yelped out the words, "Kiss him. Kiss him, Madeline."

Madeline did.

Ciaran's body relaxed and cooled down instantly.

"He can feel you. He can feel us. And that means we can feel him." Jo waved her arms in the air for victory. Madeline and Tadgh gawked.

"Can you wake him?" Tadgh asked.

Jo scurried toward the bedroom door.

"Where are you going?" Tadgh asked.

"To get the eyes." She disappeared out the door. Then they heard her voice. "I need your muscles, Tadgh."

"Oh, okay."

Tadgh rushed out of the room.

A moment later, Jo, Tadgh, Doctor Thomas, and George filed back into the room. Jo dove to the computer keyboard, doing something that only she and Ciaran would understand.

"Doctor Thomas, I need the connections to his vitals and visuals," Jo said while typing like a madwoman.

Doctor Thomas connected a wire to Ciaran's body.

"George, can you hook up the monitor?" she asked while still typing.

"My expertise." George didn't hesitate to dive in to help his cousin.

Ciaran's temperature shot up again. Madeline grabbed the cloth and wiped the sweat from his forehead. He grunted again.

"That's a fucking kick from the back. Coward," Tadgh swore.

"How do you know, Tadgh?" Madeline asked.

"I don't know, Madeline. But I have no fucking clue what else to do here."

"Done," Jo said.

George turned the monitor on. Images of faceless creatures with bodies shaped like half-man and half-ape looked back through the screen. Everyone gasped.

"Holy cow, what is that?" Tadgh gaped at the creatures.

"We're seeing what Ciaran is seeing," Jo said.

"So we are looking at this from Ciaran's perspective? We have his visual?" Doctor Thomas asked.

"Yes," Jo said.

"He's lying on the ground. Those fuckers must have attacked him from behind. Like I said, cowards!"

"Good, Tadgh, you know Ciaran's movements. Tell us—" Madeline began.

"I'd kick that fucker right there in the face," Tadgh said, pointing to the monitor.

On the monitor, they saw Ciaran's foot kick into the head of the monkey standing in the middle. The other monkeys yelped. They could see a punch here and a kick there until the bunch of monkeys retreated and ran away.

Then they saw an open field with rolling green hills on one side and stone caves on the other. The air was suspiciously still.

"What is that? Jo, is there a way we can communicate with Ciaran?" Madeline asked.

Jo shook her head. "I don't think so. I don't know how."

On the monitor, they kept seeing quiet meadows and rivers.

"No, this isn't right. It's suspicious. I wouldn't keep moving," Tadgh said.

On the monitor, the scenery became static, suggesting that Ciaran had stopped moving forward.

In the distance, they saw a pack of wolves rise from the tall grass and charge toward them.

"Oh, God, can we give him a weapon, Jo?" Madeline asked.

"It's not a hologame. I can't insert anything or manipulate the data."

"Time traveling. Is this a simulated game?" George asked.

"Can he hear us? He felt Madeline before," Tadgh said.

"I don't think he can hear any of us," Jo said.

"This is in another dimension. It's not time traveling, and it's not a hologame. It's dimensional traveling. Ciaran told me about that yesterday," Tadgh said.

"Which dimension?" Jo asked.

"I don't know. I didn't pay him any attention. Some stupid quantum physics rules. Something about a parallel universe. Some strings or wires. How the fuck should I know?" Tadgh kicked at the desk.

"You mean M theory? Quantum travel?" Jo asked.

"I don't know, Jo. Whenever he goes on about that, my brain turns into clay."

"But he's here. His body is here, at least. So whatever the dimension is, how can we channel him back here?" Madeline asked.

"Maybe you can talk him back. He can't hear us, but he seems to respond to you, Madeline," Doctor Thomas suggested.

CHAPTER 18

The ferocious wolves charged closer to savage.

Ciaran turned around and raced toward the forest. He ran as fast as he could.

On the monitor, everyone in the room could see the shaking view of the forest. They could see Ciaran's hands reaching up and breaking a tree branch. He held it like a weapon. He turned around and stared straight at the wolves.

The view of the incoming wolves filled the screen, suggesting that Ciaran had zeroed his view in and was looking straight at them.

Gigantic wolves.

They ran in a pack with structured attacking positions. The leader, an enormous black wolf, ran in the middle. It charged at Ciaran as if it was its life mission to kill him.

Ciaran stepped closer. When the wolf leaped at him, he ducked down and stabbed the sharp edge of the tree branch up. The branch impaled the wolf. It fell and roared. But the wound was not enough to kill it.

"Hit it! Whack the motherfucker into the mud!" Tadgh screamed.

On the screen, the view suggested Ciaran was doing just that. He hit at the big wolf with the tree branch nonstop.

A bunch of smaller wolves lunged at Ciaran.

"Oh my God, Jo, there are so many of them. Can we give him a gun?" Madeline asked.

"I told you before—it's not a hologame. There's nothing I can do to help. But it does feel like a simulated environment. It seems like these are challenges. Problems he has to solve to pass a test."

"Would they kill him for real?" Tadgh asked.

Before Jo could answer, Ciaran moaned.

"It must have bitten him. It did! It bit him!" Madeline yelped when she saw a streak of blood on Ciaran's hand.

Tadgh paced, mumbling to himself. "So it kills. It *can* kill."

Several smaller wolves charged at Ciaran.

"Tadgh, Tadgh . . . what would you do now?" Madeline cried out.

Tadgh still mumbled. "Don't know. I don't know. Challenge. It's a challenge. Isn't that what you said, Jo?'

"Yes," Jo responded.

"I . . . I'd try to kill the big wolf. That's my only chance," Tadgh said.

Another bleeding wound appeared on Ciaran's arm.

"They're mauling him!" Madeline panicked.

The screen filled with wolves' teeth and claws. Some were scarily close. Some of the wolves were spun away as Ciaran flailed his arms. A few more were kicked and thrown away, creating a gap.

The big wolf stood up and plunged through the gap.

Ciaran reached his hands up and grabbed for it. He spun it around and pinned it on the ground.

On the screen, it was clear that Ciaran was no longer had his weapon. His two bare hands clutched at the head of the big wolf. It tried to kick free and growled.

On the bed, another wound broke out on Ciaran shoulder.

"Crush the head! Crush its head!" Tadgh yelled.

"He can't crush that monster's head with bare hands, Tadgh," George said.

"I know. But he can't let go. It's his only chance."

Another wound broke out on Ciaran's shoulder. Blood dripped down onto the mattress.

On the screen, they saw Ciaran's hands gripped tightly on the monster's head. He was still being bitten by some of the smaller wolves, but he squeezed hard. Harder. More. But the wolf's head was still intact. It turned around and tried to bite his hands.

Madeline looked at Ciaran's face. Then looked at his hands on the screen. She understood what he needed to do—and what she needed to do to help.

On the bed now, she bent down and kissed Ciaran. Her lips connected with his. She grabbed his hands and squeezed hard.

Her thoughts connected to his.

You have my support. You have me, Madeline thought. She squeezed his hands harder. *Kill it with your bare hands, Ciaran. I love you*, Madeline told him in her mind.

With all the power of her psychic ability, she transferred her energy, her thoughts, her wishes to him.

She connected to him. This was what he needed.

Kill it, Madeline thought again.

She squeezed his hands harder. *Kill it.*

On the screen, Ciaran's hand crushed into the wolf's head. Its head caved in like a smashed watermelon.

The wolf disintegrated and vanished along with the smaller wolves.

On the screen, Ciaran looked at his hands as if he could not believe what he had done.

Madeline kissed Ciaran's cheek. She wiped the blood from the wounds on his shoulder. She wished he would open his beautiful gray eyes and look at her. But it seemed as if there were more challenges awaiting him wherever he was at the moment.

On the screen, the forest burst into flames.

Ciaran ran. He charged out of the forest and headed toward the water.

The heat must be incredible. Ciaran's body temperature shot up as if he had a fever. Madeline grabbed the cloth nearby and wiped away the sweat that dripped into his eyes.

It looked as if there was a river in the distance. He sped up. He could beat the fire.

From a small bush nearby, a baby wailed. Ciaran looked. Laurent was there, holding baby Bella in her arms, running from the fire. Laurent was lagging behind.

"It's an illusion. They want to slow him down. Come on, Ciaran. Don't stop!" Tadgh yelled.

Ciaran grabbed Bella and helped Laurent run. They slowed him down considerably. The fire caught up. It was only a few feet away from them.

Madeline knew she couldn't ask Ciaran to leave the woman and the baby behind. He had to know it was an illusion. Laurent and Bella had died in front of him weeks ago.

They were one of Ciaran's deepest regrets. They were his weakness. But still, in whatever dimension or whichever world he existed in at the moment, he could not leave the woman and the baby behind.

They approached what looked to be a river, only to discover that it wasn't a river at all. Instead, they faced a bottomless canyon, connected to the adjacent mountain by a tiny crossing bridge.

The fire exploded into fireballs, and they rolled toward them at an incredible speed. Ciaran gave baby Bella back to Laurent and helped them to the bridge. He held the bridge firmly so that Laurent could cross safely.

The fire closed in. The air pressure and the wind swung the bridge violently from side to side. The wire snapped, and the bridge collapsed.

Ciaran reached out for Laurent's hand. She dragged him over the edge of the canyon. Ciaran's left hand hung desperately onto the edge. His right hand grabbed for Laurent, who was still hanging onto the baby. They were dangling from the cliff by Ciaran's left hand which bore the entire weight of his body, Laurent's, and the baby's.

"This isn't possible. They died. It's an illusion. Let them go," Tadgh said in desperation. But he knew Ciaran would never do that.

Ciaran would never do that if it were his decision . . . if it were under his control, Madeline thought.

This was a test of the strength of a leader, of the ability to compromise and sacrifice smaller subjects for greater causes.

But this was not fair. Ciaran didn't know he was destined to be the ruler of Eudaiz. He didn't know how great of a cause it was. He didn't know this was a test. She had to help him.

CHAPTER 19

Madeline kissed Ciaran again. She locked their thoughts together. She intertwined his pain and her pain. She whispered in her mind.

Let them go, Ciaran. You have to survive.

On the bed, Ciaran's right hand grabbed at the bed sheet. Madeline held it.

Let go, Ciaran. For me. You have to survive. You have to live for me. Let go, Madeline thought.

She knew he could read her thoughts. She pulled his hand off the bed sheet. Sweat streamed down his face. Madeline could taste it. She could smell the black water at the bottom of the canyon. She could feel the breeze coming from the darkness. She could hear the call of death.

She kissed Ciaran deeper. *I love you, Ciaran. You have to stay alive. People depend on you. Let Laurent and the baby go. You have to let them go.*

Madeline pulled hard at Ciaran's right hand.

On the screen, his hand let go. The woman and the baby fell into the darkness.

A tear trickled down Ciaran's face.

Madeline wiped away the tear. She had never seen him cry. He never revealed his tears or his pain to anyone when he was in control of his body. She ached for him. In his subconsciousness, he cried for a woman and a baby who were already dead.

The screen went blank. Then it came back up.

"Where's that?" Tadgh asked.

In front of them was an endless snowfield. Nothing but white snow. In the distance, a woman stood in a white coat. She turned around.

"Mother!" Tadgh gasped. "That is total fucking bullshit. That's a trap. Ciaran will be able to tell."

"No, I don't think so." Madeline shook her head. This test was designed to target his weakness. He wasn't prepared. He didn't know. He didn't even know it was a test. Otherwise, he would treat it like a game, and he would win. This was hopeless, Madeline thought.

Ciaran approached Jennifer.

"No, no, no!" In the room, Tadgh yelled and kicked at furniture.

On the screen, Jennifer turned around and smiled. It was the gentlest, most gracious, motherly smile Madeline had ever seen from Jennifer.

Ciaran approached her.

"Jesus Christ, you're an idiot, Ciaran," Tadgh said.

Then Ciaran stopped. He looked at her from a distance.

Jennifer started to approach Ciaran. A bullet came out of nowhere and hit her. She fell to the snow. Red blood pooled, melting the snow around her.

Ciaran charged toward his mother.

Tadgh slumped to the floor. "Oh, no, no. He's done. It's a trap."

But Ciaran stopped a short distance from Jennifer. She lay in a pool of blood. She looked at him. She tried to say something to him.

The snow under his feet cracked. He looked down. It wasn't just snow. It was the ice.

A crack ran from his feet toward his mother.

She was still alive. She was looking at him. She reached her hand out to him. His mother. She would slide down into the icy water when the crack reached her.

Ciaran ran.

"No, no! Don't go near her!" Tadgh screamed at the monitor.

Madeline felt numb. She didn't know what to do.

The crack reached Jennifer.

The ice opened up, and her body slowly slid down into the dark water.

Ciaran dove, sliding on the ice toward his mother, grabbing her hand.

Jennifer and Ciaran both dropped into the dark water beneath the ice.

Jennifer's body sank to the bottom like a stone. Ciaran followed. He tried to lift her up. It was hopeless. Her eyes were glassed over. She was dead. Ciaran tried to lift the body again, but it wasn't possible to move her.

Ciaran looked up. A white light shone from the crack in the ice above through the darkness of the water.

"Go back up, go back up!" Tadgh talked to the monitor again.

In the room, Madeline gathered blankets, sheets, whatever she had on hand to cover Ciaran.

His body temperature was dropping so rapidly. It was as if he would turn to ice at any moment. He'd fail this test. She knew he would. Madeline just wanted him to stay alive. She could only hope that failing the test would not cost him his life.

She could only hope.

Ciaran was coming back up to the surface. He headed toward the light.

But the ice had closed over.

"What the fuck!" Tadgh yelled as if it would help.

Ciaran punched the ice from underneath, but it did not give an inch.

Madeline heard herself praying. No, there was no time for that. Think. She had to think.

Ciaran punched the ice again. His breath was very short now. He punched again.

On the bed, Ciaran's lips turned purple. His pulse slowed considerably.

"He's drowning," Doctor Thomas said.

Madeline thought she heard the doctor say something about drowning. Maybe not. She held Ciaran. He was as cold as ice now. He did not seem to be breathing. Tadgh was saying something, and it seemed as if there was a lot of commotion in the room. Madeline blocked all of it out.

She needed to think. She was his only connection.

What could she do? Punch through the ice block. Should she use that trick again?

Madeline kissed Ciaran's cold lips. He wasn't responding this time. She used her thoughts again.

Use my strength, Ciaran. Come back to me. Punch through the ice. You can do it.

Madeline grabbed his hands.

She squeezed them.

Nothing worked. He didn't respond.

"Come on, Ciaran," she said aloud.

On the screen, a dim shard of light drifted into the distance in space and time.

The image flickered. Flickered. Flickered. Then it went blank.

Ciaran let go. And he sank.

In the darkness, an image of Madeline appeared. She was on top of Ciaran. She was pulling him back up. He could see her face. He could see her pulling him up toward the light.

She looked at him. She smiled. She was as beautiful as an angel, coming out from the darkness. She gave him air. She kissed him. She held his body and pushed him upward.

Use my strength, Ciaran. Use my body. Come up with me.

They both moved up through the dark water toward the light. Together, their bodies punched through the ice.

It broke away like thin crystal.

In the room, Ciaran gasped and opened his eyes.

He saw Madeline's face. Still the same as it had been in the dark water. She looked like an angel. She was giving him air. She was kissing him. Her eyes were closed. She didn't need to look at him. They were connected. They had come from the darkness into the light, using their unified energy.

At this moment, they were one.

"You're very photogenic, especially when there is lust in your face, Madeline," Jo said while gawking at the monitor.

Madeline didn't register the information about the world around her. She was straddling Ciaran—the same way she had pulled him up from the dark water. She kissed him, and Ciaran held on to her.

"Hey, hey, hold on! You guys have a live audience here," Tadgh protested as Madeline and Ciaran kissed even more intensely.

Everyone hurried out of the room. They closed the door behind them.

CHAPTER 20

888

Everyone else left, but Jo stood outside the door of Ciaran's room for a little longer. She had to digest all of the information. Her head was still ringing.

The last seventy-two hours had been such a journey. War, sacrifice, death, life, love, and lust. It was truly surreal. The most bizarre thing is that the entire experience hadn't been a game. She didn't even design such weird settings for her games.

In only a few short weeks, her life and Madeline's had changed forever.

Although she'd go back to New York with Madeline soon, nothing would ever be the same. She knew Madeline would drag this out until right before Ciaran had to leave for Eudaiz. Then she'd tell him she couldn't go with him. Jo had promised not to tell.

It was awful, but she would do the same if she were in Madeline's place.

Then an image of Tadgh crossed her mind. She smiled to herself. There was something about him that made her smile whenever she thought of him. Something sweet and gentle.

Jo turned to go back to her room. While she was walking down the hallway, a door opened, and someone dragged her inside.

She was grabbed so fast that she didn't recognize who was pulling her—or to where. She fell into someone's arms.

There, she recognized Tadgh's masculine scent and his strong grip around her waist. "What in the world are you doing, Tadgh?"

"I owe you a slap in the face."

She smiled and swung her arm. She stopped her hand an inch from his face. "You really aren't going to duck?"

He grinned. "I promised you."

Madeline was right. The LeBlanc brothers should trademark their signature grins.

"All right. I forfeit my rights to claim that slap. Consider it a truce. I'm tired, Tadgh. I just want to go back to my room."

Tadgh nodded. He turned and picked up the game console she had designed for him from a side table. "I completed all the levels of the game."

She took it from him. "Impressive. Do you want the next level?"

"As long as you design the games, I'll play all of them."

"Why? You said you hated gadgets."

"But I love trying to understand how your mind works."

Shit! She stared at him. He'd hit it—her weak spot. *Damn it.* Jo turned away. "I'll design another level for you. It's going to be more difficult . . ." she said as she walked out of his room.

Tadgh grabbed her from behind. He spun her around and pressed her against the wall so fast that it knocked the breath out of her. He gazed into her eyes and sealed her lips with his kiss.

All she wanted at that moment was to surrender.

He carried her, and in a second, she was on her back in his bed. Passion pulsed out of every pore of his body. He was irresistible.

Regardless of how many men she'd been with, she'd never experienced this strong of a pull. She had always been the one in control. She would normally flip the man over and pin him down. But she lay there and took him as he came.

She tugged at his shirt and dug her hands into his taut muscles. His body was erupting with pleasure. So was hers. She could normally luxuriate in the pleasure and then walk away.

But not with Tadgh.

She stopped their kiss.

Tadgh opened his eyes and looked down at her.

She touched his cheek and tucked his hair back. "I don't do long term, Tadgh. If we do this, it's only going to hurt down the road."

Tadgh eased off her, then off the bed.

He held a hand out to help her stand up. Then he led her to the door.

"You're not going to say anything?" she asked.

He lifted her chin up and kissed her lightly on the lips. "I don't do long term, either. And you're right. This will only hurt us."

CHAPTER 21

The next morning, after a meeting with Lindsay to arrange a series of executive duties for LeBlanc Pharmaceuticals, Ciaran drove Madeline, Tadgh, and Jo to the villa outside London. They went to the villa to retrieve the disk as she had promised her grandfather.

Madeline glanced at the sky—it was as overcast as her mood. The closer it was to the time that Ciaran had to take up his duty with Eudaiz, the shorter the time she had with him. She didn't want to resent fate, but there wasn't much else she could do.

"Madeline!" Ciaran called out.

"Huh?"

"Is that the villa?"

Madeline looked to where Ciaran was pointing. The villa looked the same, surrounded by a fence of trees. "Yes," she said.

Ciaran parked at a distance from the front gate.

"It looks deserted," he said.

"Don't tell me they all died at Fountains Abbey. We didn't kill that many of them," Tadgh said from the back seat.

"The police said there were more than forty bodies in Mrs. Hanson's house. Someone must have killed all the soldiers and stashed their bodies there," Jo added.

"What was Richard like when you last talked to him?" Ciaran asked.

"As if we'd been friends forever!" Tadgh sneered.

"He said Eudaiz is a universe, not just a country or a planet. He must be looking after a lot of people . . ." Madeline's voice trailed off when a blast of metallic stench engulfed her. She glanced around. She didn't see her ghost or any blue dots.

But she had the sickening feeling that someone or something was watching her.

"Are you okay?" Ciaran tilted her chin up and looked into her eyes. Whenever he did that, she tended to give in and spill whatever she was withholding from him. She shook her head.

"I . . . just have a severe headache."

"I'll take you home as soon as we finish this." He glanced toward the house.

"How many were in the house when you were here?" Ciaran asked.

"About twenty. I think the villa looks fine . . . "

The entrance door slid open, and a man walked out.

Ciaran pushed Madeline behind him. Tadgh did the same with Jo.

The man walking toward them looked to be in his forties. He wore a dark suit that could comfortably conceal a gun. Ciaran shifted slightly. Tadgh made exactly the same move. Madeline knew they were both making sure their weapons were readied.

The man approached. "Madeline, Ciaran, Tadgh, and Jo."

"Yes . . ." Madeline said.

"I'm Lucien Hine. I replaced Douglas."

Madeline remembered vividly how Douglas, the head of the fighters, had died at Fountains Abbey.

Douglas had been kind enough to her and was a good subordinate to her grandfather.

"Mr. Hine, we're here to collect the disk as instructed," Ciaran stated.

"Yes. I've been waiting for you. Please come with me." Lucien turned and made a beeline for the house.

Inside, he strode toward a wing leading to a side door. He turned into a larger room, spacious and empty. Ciaran glanced at the setting—or lack thereof. He saw nothing suspicious.

"I'm clearing out this place," Lucien said.

"And going where?" Madeline asked.

"That's to be announced." He pointed to the cabinet. "There. I could have brought the disk to you, but Richard insisted you all come here and see the gateway. I think he meant this machine."

Lucien pressed a series of buttons on a wall panel. At the far end of the room, a wall-sized door slid open, revealing a mainframe computer unit that took up the entire width of the wall.

Rows and columns of electronic signals flashed and flowed across the screens. A control panel was located in the lower right corner. Its black glass shone, and its silver buttons were decorated with unrecognizable symbols. Madeline speculated that they were ancient symbols or some kind of language from Eudaiz.

Ciaran stood in front of the machine wall, shoving his hands into his pockets, looking at the machine as if it was a classical painting in an art gallery.

Jo gaped at the machine. "It's still operating. What will happen if we eject the disk?" Jo whispered.

Ciaran shook his head. His eyes were cool and flat. "I wouldn't take the disk now. Not until I am sure what's on it."

"How will you know what's on the disk without taking it home?" Lucien asked.

"I'll operate this machine," Ciaran said.

"It won't trigger anything, will it, Ciaran?" Madeline asked with concern.

"We're not yet ready for you to head into another dimension for another bloody training session," Tadgh said.

Ciaran contemplated. Then he turned toward Lucien.

"Who operated this computer before?"

"Juliette. At least that's what I've been told. I never met her," Lucien responded.

Tadgh rolled his eyes. Madeline asked, "Do you know what happened to Douglas? What exactly is your task here?"

"I've never met anyone in this house. It's a bit strange. I spoke to Richard via holocast . . ."

"Holocaust? What kind of communication is that?" Tadgh winced.

"No. Holo *cast*. It's an advanced communication channel that projects holographic images in augmented reality environments," Lucien spoke with authority in his voice.

"That's the funky beam of light where holographic images can walk around inside it—or jump out if they choose to. The same way Juliette kicked your ass before, Tadgh." Jo grinned.

"Nothing's funky about that beam," Tadgh grumbled.

"That's the way space stations communicate these days. I don't want to make things complicated. The technology is very advanced. My task is to give you as much assistance as I can so that you can reunite with your grandfather," Lucien said.

"Please make it simple. We're rookies when it comes to computers." Madeline smiled.

Ciaran chuckled. "We need to talk to Richard now. Would you mind giving him a call via holocast?"

Lucien shook his head. "He left this morning and won't be available for three days."

"Well, we don't want to try to operate this machine until we have more information from Richard. So we'll come back later when he's available to talk to us. Madeline can speak to him from anywhere," Ciaran said and turned to leave.

"But I have to demolish this place tomorrow. That's my job. Come on!" Lucien said.

"It will have to wait," Ciaran said dryly and walked away.

"Come on. You've seen the gateway machine. Why don't you take the disk with you? I'll turn this machine into scrap metal tomorrow anyway. Here." Lucien slammed his palm onto a gray eject button.

"Holy crap!" Tadgh said.

Ciaran and Tadgh pushed Madeline and Jo behind them. They all stared at the machine, unsure whether moving was a good idea.

The disk was ejected from the machine. The screen of the control panel flashed one line of green text: *Task completed.*

"Which task?" Madeline asked.

A number appeared on the screen, counting down by one unit per second: *six zero four seven nine nine, six zero four seven nine eight, six zero four seven nine seven* . . .

"Is that a time bomb?" Tadgh gasped.

"We're getting out of here," Ciaran said. They hurried toward the door while Lucien stood still, puzzling at the machine.

When they were at the door, the control panel flashed a red line of text: *Six zero four eight hundred.*

Lucien eventually turned and darted for the door.

They stormed outside the villa.

From a relatively safe distance, Ciaran asked Lucien, "What exactly did Richard tell you to do?"

"He said you would come and collect the disk. I had to make sure you saw the gateway before you left."

"My grandfather didn't ask you to eject the disk, did he? He wanted us to see the computer so we knew what to do and to take the disk without triggering some sort of countdown," Madeline said.

"Why didn't you say so before? Why didn't Richard make that clear?" Lucien protested.

"I don't think Richard knows about the countdown," Ciaran said. "Juliette must have coded it in."

Tadgh snorted. "He should have known Juliette better. And we have no idea what sort of bonus features Juliette may have kindly programmed into the disk."

"All right. It's my fault. I'll go in and get the disk for you," Lucien said.

"Don't do that. It might explode when you pull it out," Madeline said.

"It's a countdown to something. What's the original figure, Tadgh?" Ciaran asked.

Madeline noted that Ciaran assumed Tadgh would naturally remember the number. She was astonished when Tadgh actually remembered it.

"Six zero four eight hundred," Tadgh said.

"So what is that?" Ciaran asked.

Tadgh contemplated. "It's the number of seconds in seven days."

Jo gawked at Tadgh.

Ciaran nodded as if it was no surprise to him that Tadgh had been able to calculate the answer. Ciaran contemplated. "All right, even if it is a time bomb, we still have time. I'm going in to see if I can stop it."

"What if I'm wrong?" Tadgh asked.

"About the numbers?" Ciaran raised an eyebrow at Tadgh. "Then we won't stand a chance at anything else," he muttered and strode toward the villa. They all followed.

In front of the gigantic computer, the countdown had reduced by five minutes, the amount of time they had spent outside.

"See, you're right, Tadgh. It's a countdown by the second," Ciaran said.

"That ought to help," Tadgh muttered.

Ciaran looked at the machine for a while. Then he said, "I'm going to try something. Why don't you all leave the premises for the moment?"

There was no movement behind him. He turned around to stern stares from everyone. Ciaran turned back to the computer and typed some commands.

The monitor flashed: *Insert the disk.*

"I'm asking the computer to resume the task it was undertaking before. I'm trying to reverse the process to see if I can trick it into thinking that the disk had never been ejected," Ciaran said.

"You know what you're doing . . . you don't have to tell us, Ciaran," Jo said.

Ciaran nodded and continued typing.

The monitor flashed again: *Insert the disk.*

Ciaran shifted his left shoulder, then pushed at the disk. It slid silently inside the massive computer. The machine hummed for a second.

The monitor flashed again. *The requested task has been completed. Do you want to re-execute it?*

Ciaran shook his head. Then he said something in French. He typed in a negative command. Ciaran typed another command.

The monitor flashed: *The report is not available.*

Ciaran mumbled something else in French. Although Madeline didn't speak French, it sounded like swearing to her. When she saw a smile on Tadgh's face, she knew Ciaran was cursing out the machine.

Ciaran typed in more commands. There were more responses from the machine, but nothing useful about the task the machine had executed. At the same time, the numbers continued their countdown down by the second.

Ciaran stopped typing and thought for a moment. Then he typed again.

The monitor flashed: *The information is available. Palm print verification required.*

A square box appeared on the surface of the monitor.

Madeline stepped forward from behind Ciaran. She nudged him aside and placed her palm on the monitor. It was obvious Ciaran didn't agree with Madeline's action, but he didn't say anything.

Text flew on the monitor:
Print verified.
Madeline Kelley.
Biological age: Thirty-three.
Born in Alphi.
Citizen of Eudaiz.
Successor of Sciphil One—Richard Kelley.
Exempt from elimination.

"Exempt from elimination. What the hell does that mean?" Madeline asked.

Ciaran darted at the control panel. His fingers flew over the keyboard.

The monitor flashed: *Population of Eudaiz: six hundred and four point eight billion residents.*

Ciaran stepped back and looked at the results.

"What was the original figure on the screen before, Tadgh?"

"Six zero four eight hundred," Tadgh said with a slightly shaky voice.

On the monitor, the countdown number was six zero three nine hundred.

"It has been fifteen minutes since the original figure—that's the equivalent of nine hundred seconds. That means they are eliminating a thousand residents per second as we speak?" Tadgh said.

"What do you mean by elimination?" Lucien asked.

Ciaran shook his head. "Look at the figures and see for yourself, Lucien."

"My grandfather is killing a thousand people per second!" Madeline muttered in disbelief and stormed out of the villa.

CHAPTER 22

Ciaran charged after her. He got to her in the front yard. He pulled her into his arms and held her tightly.

"Come on, darling, calm down. I don't think Richard knew the disk would trigger the elimination," Ciaran whispered.

She tried to wriggle free, but his arms were as strong as steel shackles. When her emotions were in check, Ciaran let her go.

She called out, "Grandfather! I know you can hear me! We need to speak!"

Tadgh and Jo had followed them to the front yard.

Richard's hologram appeared. He looked as if he had aged ten years since they had last spoken.

"Grandfather, what is this elimination?"

"I swear to you—I didn't know!"

"So what *do* you know? What do you want from me, really?"

"I asked Juliette to write a program that allows Sciphil successors to access the Daimon Gate by themselves. I didn't know she had done something to the program to trigger this."

Madeline narrowed her eyes. "I don't believe you."

"Why would I want to kill the citizens of Eudaiz, Madeline?"

"You are ambitious. You want to control Eudaiz. You said so yourself."

"What good would it do me to control a universe with no inhabitants?"

"Tell us how to stop it. What's happening now in Eudaiz?" Ciaran asked.

"How can I tell you how to stop it when I don't know how it started? Juliette's program is killing people in Eudaiz. They're dropping dead by the thousands."

"You have to tell me how they're dying. Are the citizens human? If so, you have to tell me the cause of death. If they're robotic or machinelike, they can be shut down by a computer program, and I'll have a different solution for that," Ciaran explained.

"They are human-like. They're built for the Eudaizian environment. You could say that they are very fragile humans compared to those on Earth. Juliette brought something, some chemical, from Earth and is infecting them with it."

"How are they infected? Is it airborne, in the water?"

"Food. Our food is different from yours. It's a built-in system that automatically releases into the body. We program the food supply for the entire year. Juliette's program released a chemical into the food supply system. We cannot cut it off. It will take a year to reprogram."

"So either way, they'll die," Tadgh mumbled.

"What did Juliette release into the system?"

"If I knew, do you think I'd have let this happen?"

"You're saying the chemical was released. If I ask the program to resume, it might release even more of it into your system. But it wouldn't cause any more harm. I'm going to have to resume the program to know exactly what was in it."

Richard nodded. "The damage has already been done. The toxic chemical is inside the system. No more harm can be done. But if there's a way you can identify the chemical and figure out how to eliminate it, then we'd stand a chance."

Ciaran nodded. "I'll try." He turned and ran inside the house.

Inside the villa, Ciaran resumed the program. He glanced at the countdown clock and looked quickly away. Madeline stood right next to him. She knew he needed her to be right there by his side. So that was exactly where she would be.

The computer hummed and resumed its task. Ciaran typed in a chain of commands.

The monitor revealed streams of letters, codes, and symbols.

Ciaran looked at it.

He stared at it.

He turned and looked at Madeline.

Then he turned back toward the monitor. He couldn't believe what he was seeing.

He withdrew from the control panel. Madeline grabbed his hands. She sensed what was coming but could do nothing to help. She squeezed his hands. She couldn't read the computer syntax, but she knew the gibberish on the screen meant bad news.

And just to complete the terrible joke fate was playing on her, her random psychic ability let her read Ciaran's thoughts for the first time.

Madeline held Ciaran's shoulders and spun him around. "Ciaran, I love you. Listen to me, whatever happened wasn't your doing. Whatever you are going to do, please remember I love you, and I need you. Before you take any action, please think of me . . ."

Ciaran didn't seem to hear anything Madeline said. Rage was like a haze of dark matter that consumed him. She could feel his rage as much as he did. It seeded in his soul, waiting for a chance to reach out and devour him.

He shrugged off Madeline's hands and left the room. Madeline saw that her hands were shaking. She looked at Tadgh, who was waiting for her instructions. "Tadgh, please don't let him get into a car or anything."

"What the fuck is that?" Tadgh pointed at the monitor.

"Juliette used Ciaran's Golden Life formula. She tweaked it into a weapon of mass destruction and contaminated Eudaiz's food supply system," Madeline said.

Tadgh shook his head and raced out the door.

Outside, Ciaran was charging toward the car when he was tackled by Tadgh from behind. The brothers both rolled through the grass and mud.

Ciaran got up and strode again toward the car.

"You're not getting into the car. You want a one-on-one? Come on. Come here. We haven't done that in a while."

"I'm not in the mood to fight with you. Don't!" Ciaran warned. He turned around to get to the car.

Tadgh charged at Ciaran for another tackle. Ciaran swung around. In one short second, Tadgh landed on his weak ankle about fifteen feet away from his original position.

He lay on the ground, moaning.

Ciaran rushed for the car.

Jo darted toward Tadgh. She tried to help him up but couldn't take Tadgh's body weight. They both ended up on the ground. Madeline helped them both to get up.

She saw Ciaran sitting behind the steering wheel. She understood his pain. The Golden Life was his lifelong invention. With it, he'd hoped to change people's lives, to cure all diseases. Now it was being used by Juliette to cause this massacre.

She approached the car and got in. She sat next to him, saying nothing, just holding his hand. After a while, he calmed down. He got out of the car and approached Tadgh.

"Sorry about your ankle," he said to Tadgh.

"It can be fixed. No big deal. But if you drove that car away and broke your neck, I don't think I'd be able to fix you."

Ciaran grabbed his brother, bearing the weight from Tadgh's weak side. "Let's go home and find a solution to this mess." He turned toward Richard. "If I find an antidote for the chemical Juliette used, I assume that the computer in there can inject it directly into the food supply in Eudaiz?"

Richard nodded.

"So you promise not to turn that machine into scrap metal tomorrow?" Ciaran looked at Lucien.

"I'll guard it with my life."

Ciaran nodded and helped Tadgh into the car.

CHAPTER 23

Jo glanced at Ciaran. It had been twelve hours so far in the lab that he'd manned the computer mainframe. She worked on her smaller unit, but there were only limited activities she could help with.

Pharmaceutical wasn't her expertise. She could run simulations for each formula he created, but she couldn't even read the results.

Madeline entered the lab. "I need to put some food into you both."

Tadgh was right behind her. "For your info, it's pizza."

Jo sniffed the air and grinned. Tadgh approached. "Hello, green eyes. May I interest you in some slices of melted cheese on beef, chicken, sausages, sundried tomatoes, onion, and god knows what else?"

Jo laughed. "Sounds deliciously healthy."

Ciaran said nothing.

He concentrated on putting some kind of chemical extract in tubes and jars. Then he prepared two syringes, dropped the liquid in the syringes into small containers, and mixed some chemicals with the liquid. He looked pleased. He then entered the information into the computer.

Madeline approached. "If you need more time, don't push it, Ciaran. Give yourself a break."

Ciaran put the syringes down on the table. He pulled Madeline into his arms and held her. "I'm done."

"You've got it?" Madeline yelped in joy.

"Still has to be tested. I need to call Doctor Thomas."

"Why?" Jo asked.

Ciaran pointed at the two syringes—one contained a golden liquid and the other one a green liquid. "That's the Golden Life with Juliette's manipulated formula. The green one is the antidote.

I need to test them before I enter the codes into the system."

"By testing, you don't mean injecting them into yourself, do you?" Madeline narrowed her eyes. "That's why you need Doctor Thomas?"

"I have to . . ."

"You need to test the drug, and there is no time. I get it, Ciaran," Madeline stated firmly. "But if something happened to you, what do you think Doctor Thomas is going to be able to do?"

"Can we use a lab rat?" Jo asked. "I know it sounds awful, but . . ."

"The rat can't tell me what it feels, Jo. I need to monitor the drug absorption to adjust the doses of some of the key compounds," Ciaran said.

"The rat can't tell you. But I can." Tadgh grinned.

Ciaran, Madeline, and Jo turned around. Tadgh was sitting on a chair at the end of the long lab table, holding an empty syringe.

He had injected the golden liquid into himself.

"What the fuck are you doing, Tadgh?" Ciaran darted toward him, picking up the empty syringe and staring at it in disbelief.

Tadgh shrugged. "Do you want my info or not?" He stood up, but he lost his balance and fell forward. Jo grabbed him. She struggled, and

Madeline darted in to help. They lowered him down onto the lab bench.

Ciaran dragged over some equipment and connected Tadgh to the machine to get his vital signals.

"How's your breathing?" Ciaran asked.

"Fine."

"Dizzy?"

"Very."

"Vision?"

"Not good."

Ciaran typed like crazy on the keyboard.

"Scale vision from one to ten."

"Three."

Ciaran attached a drip to Tadgh's arm via a cannula. The green chemical started to drip through the transparent tube into Tadgh's system.

"Scale dizziness."

"Ten"

Ciaran altered something on the computer.

"Vision?"

"One"

"He's drifting, Ciaran," Jo said.

Ciaran made further adjustments.

"Tadgh, you hear me?"

No response.

"His pulse is rocketing, Ciaran," Jo said.

Ciaran shook his head. He made more adjustments.

"How's that, Jo?"

"Slowing down . . . too much, Ciaran."

"Now?"

"Still too low." She checked Tadgh's breathing. "He's not breathing!"

Ciaran adjusted dosage again. "Jo?"

"No. Not helping." She shook Tadgh's shoulder. "Come on. Don't do this." Tadgh was getting colder by the second. Ciaran kept typing on the computer, trying to make the necessary adjustments.

"Jo!" he called out.

"He's not breathing. Damn it." She ran to the corner and pulled the resuscitation equipment over. "You wanted to be the guinea pig . . . Well, you got what you wanted. I've never used this before," she muttered and pulled out the chargers.

Ciaran darted over and pressed a series of buttons that she assumed set it at the right level. "Do it, Jo," he said and ran back to his computer.

"No more pulse." Jo glanced at the monitor and then cranked up the machine and jolted him.

The green liquid continued to drip into his system, but there was no pulse to distribute it.

"Again, Jo," Ciaran said.

She did it again. And once more. Tadgh's body jerked up, and his vitals showed up on the monitor.

"He's back," Jo said.

"Tadgh, you hear me?" Ciaran asked.

Tadgh's body tensed. He convulsed. Jo jumped onto the bench to hold him down. His body twisted and contorted, and Jo was thrown to the floor. Madeline jumped on the bench and pinned Tadgh down.

Ciaran kept making adjustments. The convulsion eased off. He calmed down. His pulsed returned to normal. His eyes fluttered and opened.

"You hear me, Tadgh?"

"Yeah," Tadgh said groggily.

Ciaran cursed under his breath, but it was loud enough for Madeline and Jo to hear.

"Still hear me?" Ciaran asked.

Tadgh grunted out an answer.

"Vision now?"

"Ten."

"Good."

"Heart rate, Jo?"

"Perfect."

"Still dizzy?"

"Fuck yeah."

"Well, it will stay that way for a few hours. You'll just have to deal with it."

Ciaran grabbed the disk from the computer. "He can't go anywhere for the next five hours or so. Would you take care of him, Jo?"

Jo nodded. "Of course."

Ciaran checked Tadgh's pulse manually. "How are you feeling now?"

"Fine. Go away. Do whatever you have to do," Tadgh muttered.

Ciaran nodded. "I'm going to the villa to input the antidote into their system. I'll be back soon." He exited the lab with Madeline.

As soon as he heard the sound of the door clicking closed and the security system reported that Ciaran and Madeline had left the premises, Tadgh grunted and grabbed his head.

Jo held his shoulders. "Look at me, Tadgh. You're in pain. Tell me what to do. I'm going to call Ciaran."

"No, no. Don't. It has nothing to do with his antidote. I'm not in pain." He turned over to lie on his stomach and banged his head on the bench.

"Well, keep doing that and you'll soon have real pain in the head."

Tadgh sat up. She looked into his beautiful gray eyes, and all she saw there was pain. He reached over and brushed her face with his fingers.

Why did he do that? Then she turned and caught a glimpse of her face in a mirror on the door of a lab cabinet. Her eyes were red and swollen on her pale face. "All right. I must have wept a bit. But you scared the hell out of me. What's the big deal?"

He raked his fingers through his hair. "When I . . . whatever just happened now . . ."

"Like, you stopped *breathing!*"

"Yeah, whatever. Well, I was kinda like floating into darkness. I felt nothing. And then when I came back, I saw a glimpse of light. Sparks. Shapes. Voices." He looked at her now. "It's not the light that I saw, Jo. I saw your emotions."

"Right . . . so I was scared."

He shook his head. "Not just current emotions. Memories of emotions—and the results of them. I'm sorry, Jo. I didn't mean to peek into your privacy."

"No! Wait . . . no. You mean, you can see what's in my head? What I felt and what happened?" Tears came now. She couldn't control them. She'd never felt so violated.

She started to run out of the lab, but Tadgh grabbed her from behind. "I'm so sorry. I didn't mean it. I had no right to invade your privacy. But there is a part of your emotions that I am involved in. And to that extent, I'm entitled to discuss it with you."

Tadgh was too strong for her. Regardless of how much she struggled, she couldn't free herself from his grip.

"You love me, Jo. Let's face it."

"Let go of me. I have nothing to talk to you about."

"You have to love someone someday, Jo. If not me, it has to be someone."

"Let go!"

"I could see your feelings for me, loud and clear. I could see your fear. Your regrets. Your shame."

She wriggled around and punched at his chest.

"It could see your pain when it raped you. I saw the residual of its satisfaction after it was done with you. It's not human, Jo, and it wasn't your fault. I could smell the disgusting metallic stench of its satisfaction. It lived in you, and you let it—"

She broke free, turned around, and slapped him across the face.

"I'll find out what it is, and I'll kill it, Jo. . . " he snarled as she stormed out of the lab.

CHAPTER 24

The helicopter landed at the back of the villa. Ciaran and Madeline rushed to the house. Lucien was waiting for them at the door.

"Is Richard around?" Ciaran asked.

"Not now, but he will be soon."

Ciaran went straight to the computer room. Madeline knew that he deliberately did not look at the countdown clock. The number had been reduced significantly, and he didn't want to see it.

Ciaran slid the disk into the computer.

The monitor flashed:

New disk inserted. Print verification required.
Ciaran pressed his palm against the verification panel.

The monitor flashed:
Print verified.
Ciaran LeBlanc.
Biological age: 32295.24X
Born on Earth.
Citizen of the United Kingdom.
Successor of Sciphil Three—Bran LeBlanc.

"You're 32,295 years old!" Madeline said.

"No. They exaggerated. I'm only thirty thousand years old." He smiled. "They must have used a different numerical reference system. The computer is trying to convert it into something we can understand," Ciaran said while working on the commands for the program.

"Well, it's not doing a very good job. That's totally confusing!" Madeline said. "I verified before. Why did it report my Earth age?"

Ciaran paused. Then he glanced back at the computer. "The only difference I could think of is that Ayana has put a seal on my successor position, but Richard hasn't put a seal on yours."

The discussion was going in a direction she didn't care for. Madeline steered him away. "Ayana mentioned Bran is the king Sciphil, but she didn't mention he has the same surname as you. Are you related?"

Ciaran shook his head. "Unless I'm totally missing a branch of our family tree, there isn't a Bran in my family."

He executed the disk and inputted the codes into the system. Finishing the last lot of codes, he hit the "execute" button. The countdown number flashed once. Then it stopped counting down.

He nodded with satisfaction. They waited through five humming seconds. Nothing happened.

"Could you please call Richard?" Ciaran asked Madeline.

Before Madeline had a chance to call, a holocast appeared, and Richard's hologram paced back and forth in the room. He puzzled at the machine.

"I'm expecting a confirmation that the elimination has been canceled. What's happening in Eudaiz?" Ciaran asked.

"I don't know. At least it stopped," Richard said.

"That's not good enough," Ciaran muttered. "It looks as if the program paused the elimination process. But I'm not sure how long it will hold."

Richard shook his head. "I think you have to terminate the program from the source."

"How?" Madeline asked. "Didn't you said Juliette is reforming in her tower, and no one except the king Sciphil has access?"

"But you're a computer genius, aren't you? Juliette said so herself. Can you hack into her system?" he asked Ciaran.

"You want Ciaran to hack a multiversal computer system from here? I know next to nothing about computers, but that's just not possible," Madeline said.

"What exactly do I need to do to access Juliette's system?" Ciaran asked.

The computer hummed and let out a short beep. Then the countdown number started up again.

"The antidote didn't work," Ciaran muttered and mumbled some profanity.

Madeline could see Ciaran sweating with anxiety. She could feel the weight of the responsibility he'd put on his shoulders. No matter how much she tried to convince him otherwise, Madeline knew he would still take on that responsibility.

"Juliette must have used her verification code somewhere that you can hack . . ." Richard said.

"In theory, but it will take time."

The faint smell of burning electrical wiring filled the room. They looked at the computer. It looked fine. A holocast beam appeared, and the hologram of Ayana stepped forward. A corner of her long white robe had been burned off, and blood stains dampened the hem. She turned to Richard.

"Some of the Sciphils protect Eudaiz while some just take a vacation!"

"The Black Rock attacked your district because your defense is weak. Why blame me, Ayana? We're busy here. And you might not have to worry about protecting anyone in Eudaiz soon." Richard's face started to turn red.

"What do you mean?" Ayana asked. She looked at Madeline and Ciaran. "Juliette has been detained to her tower, or so I am told."

"Not just detained—they killed her presence. Now she will reform and be invincible. At the moment, she uses one of the programs to contaminate the food supply system, killing thousands per second," Richard said.

The color drained out of Ayana's face. "Only the king Sciphil can terminate Juliette. We can get Ciaran there, but that process will take a long time."

"That is if he passes the Daimon Gate alive," Richard said.

Ciaran suddenly grabbed his head and grunted in pain. "I can't hear you. Your signals are going to blow my brain out. Can you use the system?"

The control panel flashed new signals, and a line of text appeared. "Welcome, Ciaran. We are finally connected."

"Who are you?" Ciaran asked.

The monitor flashed: "I am Sciphil Three."

Ayana gasped. Madeline glanced over and saw tears gleaming in her eyes.

"Bran LeBlanc? I don't recognize your name from our family," Ciaran said.

The monitor flashed: "I am Bran LeBlanc. Consult Jennifer for the alteration of your family tree."

"Don't drag my mother into this," Ciaran snarled.

"She's already in. Go through the Daimon Gate and find out for yourself."

"Bullshit."

Ayana spoke, "Juliette is reforming in her tower and has been causing us tremendous problems. You need to terminate her, Bran."

The monitor flashed: "Can I borrow some of your energy to make contact, Ciaran?"

Ciaran was about to respond when Madeline pulled his arm.

"What exactly do you mean by borrowing his energy?" Madeline asked.

The monitor flashed: "I cannot make a physical appearance on Earth without borrowing some energy from Ciaran because he's my successor. My energy source has been disconnected."

From the back, Ayana said, "It's true. That's why he's been unable to communicate with us in the last thirty-three years. We didn't know that this connection was possible. Please help us, Ciaran."

Ayana trembled. Tears rolled down her face.

Ciaran contemplated and held his eyes briefly on Madeline. "All right, Bran."

The air thickened. A beam of light and an image appeared. This was not a hologram. This was a physical appearance from an advanced holocast. This was similar to what Juliette had used before.

Bran LeBlanc was a tall man with a kind face, white hair, and very intense gray eyes—the strongest resemblance shared in the LeBlanc family.

Madeline approached Ciaran. She wrapped her arms around his waist and could feel the energy leaking out of him in waves.

CHAPTER 25

Ciaran staggered back a few steps and then regained his stance. The appearance of Bran had sucked up a significant amount of energy from Ciaran. Madeline could feel his body weakening by the second. He was finding a point of support. She braced her body against his.

Ayana cried out loud as soon as she saw Bran. Bran gave Ayana a nod of acknowledgment. Richard stood in shock and gave Bran a stern stare. Bran was about to say something to the two Sciphils, but Madeline cut him off.

"With respect to your reunion, sir, whatever you're here to do with the borrowed energy from Ciaran, could you please do it quickly?"

Bran stepped closer to Ciaran and Madeline. He smiled. He had a genuinely kind smile, Madeline thought. The kind of smile that made her want to call him Uncle Bran.

"She's my successor. My granddaughter," Richard spoke up from the corner.

Bran's eyes brightened. "You're Madeline. You've grown up to be a beautiful young woman. It was worth it, wasn't it?"

Ciaran shifted his stance. A drop of blood trickled from his nose. Madeline tightened her grip.

"Why are you here? What can you do to stop the program?" Madeline asked.

Bran glanced at Ciaran. "You're strong, Ciaran. You resisted my full training. I hope you don't live to regret it."

"What do you need from me to stop that program?" Ciaran asked, wiping off the blood.

"You think you're responsible for what Juliette did. You hold yourself responsible for too much of what you cannot control. That's your weakness, Ciaran."

"He didn't lend you the energy to give him a lecture. So be quick, Uncle Bran." Madeline couldn't believe that had slipped out of her mouth. She'd called him uncle. A flash of a smile came across Bran's face when he heard it. He let it go.

"This is a very temporary solution. With your human energy, I can only cancel the program in Juliette's tower. The energy will not be enough for me to perform any other function. Do you understand that?"

Ciaran nodded.

Bran continued, "I know Juliette has turned against Eudaiz, and I need to end her existence. But I can no longer do it myself. Thus, you, as my successor, have to do it. To take my role as Sciphil Three and King of Eudaiz, you have to go through the Daimon Gate. I authorize Ayana to give you the induction and take you through the opening. You will not take commands from anyone but me. Am I understood?"

"And what if I fail to go through the Daimon Gate?"

Bran looked at Ciaran. "You know you won't fail. Why ask such a question?"

Ciaran nodded. He was leaning fifty percent of his weight on Madeline now, without showing the others. Madeline was glad she was tall enough to support him.

"You are using your human energy to support me to go to Eudaiz and cancel the program Juliette is running. You might not be able to recover from that loss of energy. Do you understand what you're agreeing to?"

Ciaran nodded.

"You're a brave man, Ciaran. I am pleased. This will only take ten seconds."

Bran nodded at Ayana and Richard and beamed off. As soon as he swooped out of the room, all six foot three inches of Ciaran collapsed to the floor.

Tears rolled down Madeline's face.

Ciaran looked at her. "Come on, darling. I'm not hurt. I just don't have any strength at the moment. Don't cry. I can't even wipe the tears off your pretty face." He smiled.

Madeline brushed away her tears and forced a smile. "I'll keep a lookout and make sure no one comes to beat you up now."

Madeline removed a strand of hair from Ciaran's face. "Promise me you won't agree to anything else?"

"Okay."

The ten seconds went past. Bran came back to the room.

"Successful?" Madeline asked.

"Trivial. I canceled Juliette's program. And I had a quick look around before I left. Her reform is progressing very fast."

"How fast? How long before we need to cut off her energy source?" Ayana asked.

Bran crouched down next to Ciaran. "You understand that you will take on the Sciphil Three position and that you will be the one who ends Juliette?"

"Yes."

"We won't have much time. Two weeks top before she regains her form. Ciaran has to pass the gate before that. When and where is your next opening, Ayana?" Bran asked.

"Australia. In ten days, Earth time," Ayana said.

"Why?"

"My successor is Zach Flynn. He's an Australian."

Bran nodded. "Fair enough. Good successors are hard to come by. I trust your judgment."

"He's strong, fair, and talented," Ayana responded.

Bran spoke to Ciaran next. "Ayana's gate will be yours, Ciaran. Before I go, there is one last thing I would like you to consider."

Madeline's body tensed up. This couldn't be good news.

"And that is?" Ciaran asked.

"The chemical in your body, the Golden Life, it was not meant to be there. Your mother put it in there. I know that. But you are better off without it."

Madeline raised her voice. "No, no, you don't understand Bran. He died. Ciaran died in front of me. If Jennifer hadn't injected him with that chemical, he would have been gone. I saw it with my own eyes . . ."

"He can survive . . ."

"No, I said no. Whatever you're suggesting, the answer is no. Now, you piss off and go back to where you came from. Give Ciaran his energy back."

"What are you suggesting?" Ciaran asked.

"No, Ciaran, you promised me. You didn't see yourself dying. I did. I won't go through it again. You go away, Bran. No more talking. You saved the people of Eudaiz. Please leave."

"What are you talking about, Bran?" Ciaran asked again.

"I won't forgive you, Ciaran, for doing this to me again. I swear to you." Tears streamed down Madeline's face. She knew what was coming. She knew she couldn't stop it.

Bran looked at Madeline, and then he looked at Ciaran. "I can purify that chemical out of your body. Nobody else can do this for you. You're strong. You can survive without it. This way, you don't owe anything to anyone."

"No, he can't. He was shot. He died in my arms!" Madeline cried.

"You have a very strong will. You can survive. If I go now, you will not have the energy to get me back here to perform that function for you. It will be in your body forever. You will owe Juliette forever . . ."

"If you do this, I will not forgive you whether you survive it or not, Ciaran," Madeline said in tears.

"Then get rid of it," Ciaran said to Bran.

Madeline sobbed.

"This is an equivalent to level one of the Daimon Gate. The purification process is not a big deal. You can pass it easily. But this procedure will return you to the stage just before the time you received the chemical. You will be very weak. Another risk is that I have to use your energy now to perform that function. It will weaken you even further. I think you are strong. But the risks cannot be ignored. Are you sure this is what you want?"

Madeline scrambled to leave the room.

"Madeline!" Ciaran called out. "Please stay with me."

Nasty son-of-a-bitch, she cursed silently as she sat down next to him.

"I'll take my chances, Bran. Do it," Ciaran said.

"Remember what you promised me when you refused my training, Ciaran. I am holding you to it."

Ciaran nodded.

Bran grabbed Ciaran's wrists. Ciaran's body jerked up as if he had been electrocuted. His body glowed and gradually turned almost transparent. Then it returned to a solid state.

In front of a devastated Madeline, Ciaran fell flat on the floor. He was no longer conscious. A satisfied smile crossed Bran's face. He turned around and disappeared the way he had come.

Madeline dumped the contents of her purse looking for the phone. She grabbed the phone and shouted into it, "Doctor Thomas!"

CHAPTER 26

"**J**o! Come back!" Tadgh yelled after Jo. She had called the taxi and had cleared her way out of Mon Ciel. The door slid open, not for Jo to go out but for Doctor Thomas's car to come in. In the sky, the helicopter hovered and landed in the front garden.

"Trouble," Jo muttered. "When can I get the hell out of here?" She turned back and saw that Tadgh had rushed over to the helicopter transporting Madeline and Ciaran.

She turned and was about to follow everyone inside the house to check on Ciaran when she saw a ghost standing outside Mon Ciel. Jo squinted.

Outside Mon Ciel's fence, the image of the old man, Larry, stood. *The ghost from ten years ago in Australia? He'd come back?*

She couldn't believe this. She had never seen a ghost before. She wasn't the psychic—Madeline was. The man had died—and she didn't believe in ghosts.

The image flickered and changed into something else. It was now a demon, the kind that only appeared in her hologames. A metallic stench engulfed her.

She looked toward Mon Ciel and saw Tadgh looking at her. He had read into her emotional reactions. This newfound ability of his was going kill their relationship. At least it would from her end.

Jo ignored the image and walked toward the house.

They were taking Ciaran inside. Madeline was so focused on him, she wouldn't see anything else. But then Jo saw Madeline pause and turn to look toward the gate where the ghost had just stood.

Madeline frowned then turned to enter the house.

Jo felt to be sure the gun Ciaran had given her was still inside her jacket and walked toward the house.

***

Half an hour later, Jo stood in the back garden admiring the headless statue of the Goddess of Kindness. Madeline had told her the story of the statue once. Ciaran had blown its head off when he had experimented some chemical compound when he was only four.

Jo shook her head. Madeline loved Ciaran so deeply. She understood why. But the whole thing was still surreal to her.

And now Tadgh and her feelings for him.

It was seriously time for her to leave.

The door to the back garden slid open, and Madeline strode out.

"How's he doing?" Jo asked.

Madeline was startled but composed herself quickly. "He won't be moving for the next day or so. But apart from that, he's fine. I needed to talk to you, Jo."

"By sneaking out through the back gardens? You're going to leave Ciaran now, aren't you?"

"I . . ."

"How are you going to get out of the gate without alerting security?"

Madeline shrugged as if she hadn't planned that far in advance.

"Okay, let's go."

"What?"

Jo dangled the car keys in front of Madeline. "Tampering with the security system from the inside is child's play for me, especially when Ciaran is down. Nobody will catch us."

Madeline nodded, and they both darted toward the garage.

Five minutes later in the car, Jo smiled. "I didn't know you had tachophobia like Tadgh."

"I don't have an issue with speed, but this isn't exactly the right time for you to be driving fast. You're worse than Ciaran when he's mega mad." Madeline braced herself against the passenger seat.

"Well, he will be apocalyptically mad when he finds this out."

"I don't have a choice. But you do. Why are you leaving Tadgh? You obviously like him."

"The stupid drug he injected himself with gave him the ability to see people's emotions. He saw my emotions from Australia, and he's not going to be fine with it."

"I'm sorry about that, Jo."

"Madeline, it's been ten years. I'm no longer eighteen. Shit happened. And I've grown out of it. Even if it raped me—"

"What? I thought he tried, but he couldn't."

"It wasn't Larry. You know what I'm talking about, Madeline."

Madeline narrowed her eyes. "No, I don't."

"Larry was being controlled. He was possessed. You said so yourself."

"Yes. And because of that, he's innocent. When I killed him, I killed an innocent man."

"There are no ghosts or spirits, Madeline. What controlled Larry was a mind bender. People who can control other people's minds. It took me a long time to come to terms with it."

"Stop the car, Jo. Stop it. Now you sound like Ciaran."

"Yes. I sound like him." Jo stopped the car and stormed out. "And for your information, we agreed that you should tell me what exactly you did. Not just 'I might have killed an innocent man.'"

"Ciaran knew?"

"Not yet, but I'll tell him. Ghosts don't rape live people. But it raped me, Madeline. I can still smell his metallic stench on me."

"Oh, Jo! I'm so sorry. You never told me."

"Told you what? A mind bender forced his mind on me and mentally raped me? I don't know how it worked. I just knew when I was violated."

Tears rolled down Jo's face now. "I can still smell him. I would have rather it made Larry rape me because at least then I could have fought back."

"It's not just the one incident. It's a ghost. Believe me. It's haunted me for years. Remember all the records of violent crimes I committed when I was younger that you erased for me? It made me do those things."

"It possessed you?"

"No. It possessed men around me to kill and rape everyone around them and then kill themselves. It told me that. It's haunted me since I was ten. And it told me that if I didn't kill the men it possessed, it would keep killing. My only solution was to knock the men out. But it'd never forced itself on any women."

"Until me?"

"Maybe. I don't know, Jo. I just saw it in front of Mon Ciel before. I thought I had killed Larry, and it had let me be in peace. I don't know why it came back."

"I saw it, too," Jo muttered. "But I don't believe it's a ghost. Mind benders are humans. As long as it has blood and flesh, it will just have to deal with me now, once and for all."

Madeline suddenly grabbed Jo and shoved her toward the back. "It's here."

"I can smell it." Jo pulled out her gun.

Madeline stepped toward the front and pulled out a knife she had tucked inside her jacket.

The metallic stench filled the air.

But they saw no one.

An image flickered in front of them, and something in the shape of a man appeared. "It's the middle of the damn day . . ." Jo grunted and shot at the creature.

The bullet shot through the image and kept going.

The image appeared a bit more solid, and the ancient, ugly face of an old man started to form. He smirked at them.

Jo shot again. The same thing happened. The bullet tore through thin air.

"It's not human, Jo. I told you." Madeline charged at the image and swung her knife. It disappeared.

They heard car engine roaring in the distance.

"Oh, no," Jo moaned.

"When a guy with tachophobia drives like that, it tells you just how much he cares about you. But we can't let him come near us, Jo. The ghost possesses men."

Tadgh's car fishtailed and stopped right next to theirs. He stormed out, yelling. "Where do you think you two are going?" He walked for a couple of steps and started to stagger. His eyes became bloodshot.

"Oh no!" Madeline cried and darted toward Tadgh. Before he could do anything awful, she used her knife handle to whack him in the temple, knocking him out cold on the ground.

Madeline turned around, looking at Jo. "Now you've seen it firsthand, Jo. It wants me, and there's no other way to handle this."

Madeline strode toward the car, got in, and drove away.

CHAPTER 27

London streets were the same. Londoners were the same. Morning rush. Traffic. Winter breezes. Madeline did not expect that London would have changed much in the last few weeks. It was still winter. The sun still came out late in the morning.

The days were still short, and the darkness still occupied a large part of the daily cycle. People still worked for a living. Life in London went on with or without what happened in Eudaiz, another universe. Soon, this London scene would be history to her.

She thought about Ciaran. She allowed herself a moment to think of him. She thought she would think of him for the rest of her life.

This morning, Jo had messaged her and said Ciaran had regained ninety percent of his strength, according to Doctor Thomas. She trusted that, with Jo's skill, her message wouldn't be tracked.

Madeline still resented the joke fate had played on her. Even with a standby, she couldn't get a flight to New York until tomorrow. She was lucky they could schedule her at all.

She finished off her coffee and headed toward the British museum. She wanted to take a look at John Dee's glass again for no particular reason. It might be the last time she got to see it, and it had marked a significant stage in her life. Why not?

The museum was quiet but not lacking visitors. Madeline found the glass again. It sat there just as it had for the last five hundred years.

The air thickened. Madeline was into this holo-techno enough now to know that she was entering a holo-communication sphere. A holographic image of Ayana appeared. Ayana was careful enough to block the view from other visitors so that they could not see the holo-communication.

"I thought it was my grandfather," Madeline said.

Ayana smiled. Her blue eyes pierced through the thickened air to cast a warm look at Madeline. "I understand that you left Ciaran."

"He told you? Or were you stalking me as soon as I left Mon Ciel?"

"The latter, Madeline. Do you think Ciaran would storm out to the field to tell me that you left him?"

"Of course not. What can I do for you? As you can see, I no longer want to be associated with this whole ordeal. I will explain things to my grandfather."

"I'm afraid it won't be so simple."

"Okay, I broke my promise to grandfather. He'll be mad at me. So smite me—or whatever you have to do. I'm going back to New York tomorrow. No one can do anything to stop me."

"Including Ciaran?"

"Yes."

"You're being unfair, Madeline. Ciaran didn't have a chance to talk to you."

"I have had enough of this."

"You're clear-headed. You have a strong mind. I think you would serve Eudaiz well. I'm not speaking for Ciaran. I'm speaking on behalf of the Eudaizian people who will need you in the future."

"I'm sure you can do without me. I'm going back to New York. Let me be an ordinary person."

"You were born in extraordinary circumstances. You were conceived in Eudaiz, like me. But you spent your life on Earth. You can never be ordinary, Madeline. You don't know what it has taken for you to be able to stand here talking to me like this. You don't know what or who has paid for your well-being."

"You're blackmailing me?"

"If you say so. I will do what I must. That's the least I can do for your grandfather. He is ambitious and manipulative. But his concern for Eudaiz is genuine."

"What happened to my grandfather?"

"The Black Rock is our utmost enemy. Richard's district was attacked several times. That was why Richard formed an alliance with Juliette and sought the sample gold from the LeBlancs. He was developing a weapon that could destroy the Black Rock. But that weapon cost a lot of resources and lives. He hasn't gotten anywhere with it—you know the situation with Juliette. Now he's under attack and has no weapon."

"What can I do? Can't you help?"

"I can help Richard within my limits. But I have to take care of my district first. Richard has created a lot of enemies and alienated many other Sciphils because of the way he operates. It doesn't do him any favors now. The most important mission of a Sciphil is to have a ready successor. If you leave Richard now, he will have no chance of finding another one."

"Is he injured?"

"I'm not sure about his current status. But I know he will need you very soon. I don't think he could even open the gate for you now. He is very weak."

"What do you suggest I do?"

"Go back to Ciaran. Go with him to Australia. I will let you go through my opening, provided I have Richard's permission to do so."

Madeline shook her head. "I've killed an innocent man. My soul is not virtuous—I can't pass the Daimon Gate alive. There is no point in my grandfather trying to get me there."

Ayana nodded. "He will have to pay for this dearly."

"How? What do you mean?"

Ayana shook her head. "Richard has decisions to make. I can't speak for him. But, in any case, if you need to go through the gate, I am happy to take you to the opening together with Ciaran. Goodbye for now." Ayana smiled, and the hologram disappeared.

Madeline left the museum. She walked along the streets, heading back toward her hotel, wallowing in thought. She should stick to her plan. She should talk to her grandfather, Madeline mused. Whether she desired it or not, he was her family, the only family she knew.

Madeline realized that for the first time in her life she felt like an orphan.

She had been a fighter. Shuffled from one foster care home to another. Growing up, making a career and a life for herself. Then Jo came along. She loved Jo's family and adopted them as her own. Maybe her life had been so full that she had never had a chance to think about her biological connection. She'd never thought of herself as a victim or an orphan.

Why now?

It was when she'd found her biological family that she'd felt lonelier than ever.

Madeline had arrived at her hotel before she knew it. As soon as she entered her room on the sixteenth floor, she knew something was not right.

She wanted to leave the room, but she couldn't open the door. It seemed to weigh a ton. Her window was open, letting a blast of cold air inside. The breeze cut into her skin. As much as she would like to deny her sixth sense right now, she could not dismiss the nauseous feeling she had.

It was him. Her ghost. In the room.

CHAPTER 28

Madeline turned on all the lights in the room and slammed the window shut. The room warmed up instantly. Too warm. She heard the click of the door lock. She charged toward the door and opened it. She could run and escape the hotel. Be seen in public. Then there would be nothing he could do to her.

But she was not a coward. She refused to run. He wouldn't appear for no reason. What was it he wanted?

Madeline re-entered her room and closed the door.

"I know you're here. Come out. Tell me what you want. Don't be a coward."

Nothing happened.

"I know you're here. I can sense you. You know that, right? Whatever you're waiting for in here is not going to happen because I'm leaving now."

Nothing.

"Chicken," Madeline mumbled and went to the bathroom. She filled the sink with water and poured all of the bottles of shampoo, conditioner, lotion, and gel she could find into the water and dissolved them. They made a light-colored bubbling tub of water. She scooped up some water with a small hotel glass and started splatting it everywhere.

She kept doing so until the water hit a form. "Got you, bastard," she said.

She dropped the glass instantly and grabbed a chair. She flew over the bed and swung at the form where she could still see some water on it.

It roared, the low rumbling roar of a beast.

Madeline kept swinging and hitting. She knew it couldn't hurt her. For more than a decade, it hadn't changed its ways. It would not hurt her directly. It would have to borrow a human form to do so. But there was no one else in the room for it to manipulate. So Madeline continued her attack without fear.

It roared again and again, whenever Madeline hit it. But it would not run away as it had before.

The air in the room thickened, an obvious sign of a coming holocast. "Not now, for God's sake," Madeline thought.

A beam of light appeared, and the holographic image of Richard formed.

"Poor timing, Grandfather. I know we have to talk, but not now and not here."

Richard stared in confusion at Madeline, who was in combat stance on the bed, holding a chair with both arms.

"I've never done you harm, Madeline."

"Not you! Just not now. Please go away, Grandfather."

Madeline gauged the room. The marks of water were gone. She could not see the form of the beast now. If there were another person present, the beast would have manipulated the person's mind to attack Madeline. That was its usual *modus operandi*. Unfortunately for the beast, Madeline thought, Richard was a hologram, and could not attack her physically.

The room was quiet. Madeline could not sense the beast anymore. If it was still there, it had somehow suppressed all of its energy.

A moment went past. Another moment. And still nothing happened.

Richard looked puzzled.

Madeline put the chair down. When she finally had a chance to look at Richard, she cried, "Holy Jesus Christ, how bad are you hurt?" His clothes were covered in blood.

She darted toward the hologram only to realize that she couldn't touch him.

"I'm injured. But the majority of the blood is not mine. Don't worry, I can manage."

Madeline puffed out a breath. It was probably not a good time to tell him she did not want to be a Sciphil anymore.

"What can I do for you now? Ayana told me your district is under attack."

Richard smiled. "It was very kind of her. She is a good woman no matter what side she is on. What else did she tell you?"

"That you're in trouble, and that you might need me."

Richard sneered. "Since when am I in trouble? And who is she to judge?"

"She wasn't judging. She simply wanted to help. I'm leaving Ciaran. I wanted to get out of the whole Eudaiz ordeal, and that's why she told me that you might need me. Now you're telling me you don't need any help. So that's great. I'm free to go back to New York then."

Richard's eyes drooped. He shook his head. He didn't have to say it—Madeline could see that he was in deep trouble. The man had his pride. Just like Ciaran—choosing possible death over having Juliette's drug in his system.

Damn it, Madeline cursed silently.

"Would you come to Eudaiz and help me?"

"You want me to be right next to you, ready to take the Sciphil role if anything should happen to you, right? Is it really that bad?"

Richard drew in a long breath, then nodded. "I made a mistake. It was too late to recover. I might never recover. So yes, it's bad, and I need you to be ready. I have to take you through now. I might not have another chance at this."

"My soul is not virtuous. I have killed an innocent man. The Daimon Gate will kill me."

"What happened?"

"There is a creature. It haunted me through all of my childhood. It said it would continue to kill people until I killed one of the innocent men it possessed. Don't ask me why. I don't know. The creature was here just before you came. I thought it had left me after I killed that man in Australia. But for some reason, it's come back."

"What creature? What are you talking about?"

"I told you I don't know. And I don't know how to solve this situation. But I can't come with you to Eudaiz."

"There had to be a way," Richard said.

"Maybe there is. But I don't want to waste your resources, chances, or energy. If you have a choice better than me—"

"I don't have anyone else, Madeline. You're the only family I have left. I would never leave this role to an outsider."

"You might have to if I die during the process."

"I won't let anything happen to you, Madeline. I lost you once. Never again. If I don't have a successor, I'll let my eudqi collapse."

"You'd let Eudaiz be destroyed?"

"I would rather it be destroyed in my hands than in someone else's. I don't know who to trust anymore. The Black Rock is evil. They have many forms. If they took over Eudaiz, it would be a fate far worse than death for the citizens."

Madeline nodded. "So what's the solution?"

"There are different routes to take, and there is one I know of that could work. I won't risk you going through it, though, before testing it. So I'm going to get you inside the gate for the test. Are you afraid?"

"No, of course not."

Richard nodded. "We'll go from here."

"What? You mean you can open the Daimon Gate right here? I thought it was huge."

"Opening the gate is very significant. But this is just a test. I'll see if I can push it."

He concentrated for a moment. His image glowed as if he were transforming from a hologram into a real presence. Madeline could feel the energy radiating from him. The circle of light around him—which used to be the holocast—expanded and brightened.

The circle illuminated in blue and white and grew even more. Madeline felt the energy growing as if Richard were moving closer to her. She shifted, suddenly not sure she was ready. But it was a call to duty, she might as well just do it.

Richard reached his hand out. "Give me your right hand."

Madeline obeyed. Richard held it. She felt his presence and the waves of energy coming out of him like little electrical currents.

The hotel room was small, but when the circle of light reached a corner, Madeline saw an unusual bend in the light. She could see the shape of the beast hiding in the corner.

"Stop, stop!" Madeline yelled at Richard.

Richard stopped the circle.

"Can anyone go through the gate when you open it?"

"Yes, Madeline. But I cannot hold it for long. What is it?"

"The creature is here, in the room. Can it get through the gate?"

"Yes. But a gate-crasher will be killed on exit. Let it come in. I'll kill it now to save time."

Richard expanded the circle further.

For the first time, Madeline could see the creature in full view. It was truly a beast. The light from the circle shined on it. It stood. It had a shape like that of an ape, and its head nearly reached the ceiling.

Richard could see it now.

"Stop!" Madeline yelled again. She grabbed the chair and attacked the beast as she'd done earlier. It seemed totally unaffected by her blows.

Richard stopped the circle of light. He looked at the beast as it approached him. His eyes registered some recognition.

"Kyle Wolf, you traitor!" Richard grunted out the words, his face glowing with a strange combination of astonishment and fury.

"Richard!" The beast croaked out his name in a disembodied voice that came straight from hell. "I have come to see you fail and to claim what you promised." It paused for a moment and then roared and reached its hands out to grab Richard.

Richard staggered back to avoid the creature's grasp. He was not a hologram now. He was on the verge of opening the gate, and he had revealed his presence.

Madeline hit the control panel for the ceiling fan. It whirled at the beast's head. The hit was not hard enough to do damage, but it served as a distraction.

"Go!" Madeline screamed at Richard.

Richard withdrew the light and vanished.

CHAPTER 26

The beast turned around. Its body was still glowing. It was a gigantic ape. It slapped at Madeline with the back of its fist, throwing her against the wall.

Madeline was nearly knocked unconscious. She scrambled up and realized that the beast had gotten smaller and looked more like a werewolf now. Madeline deduced that whenever it attacked her directly, it grew smaller and weaker. That was why it had never touched her before.

Madeline charged at the wolf now for a one-on-one. She attacked with all that she had—fists, legs, fingernails. She tried to cause as much damage to it as possible before it became invisible to her again.

The wolf roared in pain and fled to the hallway. Once there, it became invisible.

Madeline ran out of the room. She saw a pregnant woman walking toward her with two toddlers in tow. Suddenly, the woman's eyes rolled up in her head. She let go of the toddlers and charged at Madeline.

"Oh, great!" Madeline muttered. "You've hit an all-time low . . . A pregnant woman? You scumbag!" Madeline stepped backward, trying to talk to the woman.

"Don't come near me! Go back to your sons. They're crying." She knew this wouldn't work. The only way to get the beast out of the woman was to knock her unconscious. Madeline had done that before. She knew what she was doing.

Madeline dodged to the side. The woman lost her momentum, and at that moment, Madeline snatched a vase and hit her. The woman fell to the floor, but she got up quickly.

Madeline plucked up the two wailing toddlers, carrying them in through the exit door. The woman stood, looking at Madeline. She didn't attack.

Instead, she grabbed the handle of a door next to her and pulled. She broke the door with her bare hand and entered what looked to be a control room of some kind.

"Oh, no . . ." It was too late for Madeline to do anything. She didn't have the strength to go against the woman. She carried the toddlers quickly down the emergency exit stairs.

Madeline fled out into the foyer of the hotel. She shoved the toddlers toward the concierge. In the corner of the foyer was a sign saying "Conference Main Hall" with an arrow pointing to a wing.

Madeline ran up a flight of stairs to the main hall of the conference wing. She entered the conference and galloped up to the stage. The presenter was talking about global warming or something like that. The gigantic PowerPoint screen was flashing images of forests, animals, and oceans accompanied by a host of diagrams and figures.

Now I look like a lunatic, she said to herself.

She snatched the microphone from the presenter and glanced down the hall toward the few hundred people in the audience.

Someone to the side of the stage was alerting security. They entered the hall, approaching the stage.

"My name is Madeline Roux. I'm a journalist from New York. I am asking you, for your safety, to exit this hall right now. Exit this building right now. Don't panic. Don't scramble. But leave, please."

Silence.

Security approached the stage. The crowd was not moving.

"Oh, for God's sake. There's a bomb in the building," she lied. "Run now if you want to live."

And the chaos began.

Madeline threw the microphone at the approaching security guards and rushed toward the backstage. On her way out, she saw a fire alarm box. She smashed the glass with her elbow and pulled the alarm.

Madeline ran to the main entrance. A good number of people had already gotten out of the building. Alarm bells rang everywhere.

But nothing was happening.

Shit, Madeline thought.

Across the hallway, a group of security officers gathered. One of them pointed at her. Madeline ran from the building.

As soon as she had gotten past the door, she could hear and feel it—the rumbling sound of a fireball hurtling down from the sixteenth floor.

The ground was shaking. The building went down.

She ran further and further away, and then she was drowning in dust and darkness.

CHAPTER 30

Madeline didn't know how long she had been lying still in the dark. She could hear herself breathing, but she found it hard to breathe in the dusty air. She drew another breath. It was difficult. She tried to say something but couldn't.

Someone handled her. She was lifted, pulled, poked. Someone else gave her some air. That made the breathing easier. She was still in the dark, though. She thought she heard a familiar voice. Ciaran's voice. Maybe. Maybe not. She drifted off again, into the darkness.

Madeline came about a little later. She opened her eyes to see a white ceiling. She was in a real hospital room judging by the equipment around her. She took a mental inventory.

She didn't feel much pain. A drip was attached to her arm. She moved a little on the bed. Everything felt fine. She could wiggle her toes. Perfect. Intact. She could feel all ten and could see her four limbs still attached to the right places on her body.

Madeline pulled herself up. That felt okay, too. She hitched herself up again. Good. She looked around. By the looks of it, it was a private hospital room. There was a small TV in the corner of the room. Madeline grabbed the remote control on the side table and turned it on.

She was not surprised to see scenes of the hotel disaster flashing on the breaking news. But her jaw dropped when she saw Ciaran giving a press conference.

Her Ciaran, calm and collected. His gorgeous face looked straight at the screen. He looked as if he was talking directly to her. Madeline didn't know what time it was or how long it had been. But by that morning, Ciaran was supposed to have gotten ninety percent of his strength back. Now he looked as if he had only fifty.

A reporter asked, "Mr. LeBlanc, could you confirm that the LeBlancs will donate all medical equipment and pay for the expenses of the treatments for the victims at the hotel today? You said so at the scene."

"Yes. It won't be the first time we have made donations to medical causes."

"But this is the first time the LeBlancs have made a public announcement. What's different about this incident?" another reporter asked.

"Madeline Roux is a good friend of mine. As you flashed her name all over the media, I felt the need to address some of the questions myself."

"The witness said she knew about the explosion."

"She saved a lot of lives because she warned people. If she had any involvement in it, she would have given herself a safer distance from the explosion, wouldn't she? If you want to waste your time speculating, feel free to do so, but do not waste my time."

"You were seen at the police station with her a few weeks ago. Is there a connection between that incident and what happened this morning?"

"No." Ciaran stared hard at the reporter. The reporter withdrew his next question.

"How do you explain the LeBlancs' involvement at the Fountains Abbey fight, where many people were killed?"

Ciaran glanced at the reporter who had asked the question. "Which of us did you see there?

"The report stated that . . ."

"I don't care what your report said. If you want to make such an accusation against our family, you'd better have proven facts. Once you have these facts, make an appointment and talk to my lawyers. Twenty people died today. I will only take questions about how to help these victims and their families and how to help the business get back on its feet. If you think you can use this opportunity to dig up some dirt on my family, you are sadly mistaken."

Madeline turned the TV off. She knew how it went. This used to be a part of her life. Now it was being used against her. She could handle the media and the scandal. But she could not bear seeing Ciaran's face. She didn't know seeing him would hurt so much. She didn't even know why it hurt.

She felt tired now. She put the remote away and tried to reach for the water. A nurse saw her from the outside and hurried in.

Ciaran was right behind.

The nurse gave Madeline the water and some meds. She checked on vitals.

Ciaran usually did all of that. Doctor Thomas was the only medical professional that Ciaran would allow when it came to her. But now, Ciaran stood in the corner of the room, watching the nurse working on her. He stood there with his hands jammed in his pockets. Like an acquaintance of hers.

The nurse finished and left the room.

Ciaran approached. He sat beside the bed. It felt as if he was sitting a mile away.

"Lindsay saw you on the news. He called me."

"I guess I'm famous now. Or infamous."

Ciaran smiled. "I don't care about reputation. You should know that by now. Or you might not . . . Your documentation was destroyed at the hotel. I regret that you won't make your flight tomorrow. But I can make arrangements for you at your earliest convenience . . . if you like."

His words felt like a knife in her heart.

Ciaran squeezed her hand slightly. "The doctor said you were noncritical four hours ago. You can go whenever you want. I figured you wouldn't want to go back to Mon Ciel. So I arranged this private room. I hope you don't mind."

Madeline said nothing. It was so damn polite of him. She would rather he kicked and screamed. She could handle flash rage. She had so much to tell him. But that wasn't the issue. The issue was that she wanted to tell him so much. She missed talking to him. At this pace, she would probably die of old age before she could tell him anything.

"I could get Jo to come stay with you. Whatever you like. Tell me what you want."

Madeline looked at the circles under Ciaran's eyes. She wagered he had about forty percent of his energy left. Going backward from ninety this morning.

Madeline cursed herself for doing such a good job. Maybe she should get him back to zero percent, the way he was at the villa, and then he'd miss the Daimon Gate in Australia. Then the billions of people, people who would be enslaved or killed in Eudaiz, would worship her statue in a monument!

"Madeline, what would you like me to do?" Ciaran asked.

Madeline opened her eyes. A tear trickled down her face. Then another.

"I need a moment by myself," she said.

Ciaran nodded. "I'm sorry. I didn't realize I had caused you so much pain. I am terribly sorry." He walked to the window and stood looking outside.

"Ciaran."

"Yes? I'm leaving now." He turned around and walked toward the door as if he were leaving. His deep gray eyes were intense, and his face was unfathomable—his usual Ciaran look.

"You have your secret gun with you?"

Ciaran glanced at the door. "Yes."

"Can I borrow it?"

"What?"

"I don't even think guns worked on it."

Madeline slid down under the blanket, pulling it over her head and sinking her head into the pillow. Ciaran darted toward the bed. He touched her shoulder. "Madeline, are you in pain? Should I call the doctors?"

Madeline turned, lying on her back. Ciaran pulled the blanket down to see her face. Big tears rolled down from her eyes. He wiped them away. It was rare for Madeline to see Ciaran looking this stressed.

"Where does it hurt? I'll call the doctors."

More tears rolled down her face.

"I'm sorry, darling. Please don't cry. I won't do it again."

"You won't do what again?"

"I . . . I . . . You tell me what I did wrong, Madeline."

Oh, great, her British lover was apologizing even though he didn't know what he did wrong.

Madeline pulled at Ciaran's hand. "Would you lie down with me for a minute?"

Ciaran complied.

Madeline rubbed her thumb over the circles underneath his eyes. Down to thirty percent of energy now, her king, her hero. She ought to fix it. She reached over and kissed him.

Ciaran resisted the kiss. "I've never wanted to hurt you. If you tell me what I did wrong, I'll fix it," Ciaran told her.

"I love you, Ciaran."

"So why did you leave me?"

"I can't go with you through the Daimon Gate..." She curled into his arms. There, she told him everything.

"There has to be a way out of this," Ciaran said.

She shook her head. Suddenly, she sensed the beast again. She shot up in the bed, glancing around.

"Is it here?" Ciaran asked.

"Yes. Get away from me, Ciaran. It possesses people. Please go away, Ciaran."

She tried not to stutter, but fear had occupied every corner of her mind now.

She was scared.

She had never been scared of the beast before. She sensed that it was going to do something she hadn't dealt with before. Something with more severe consequences. She feared that the beast was not just a beast. It was something a lot more than that.

Her grandfather had called it Kyle Wolf. Her grandfather knew it and had promised it something it had come to claim.

The air in the room grew cold quickly.

Ciaran jumped off the bed and pulled out his gun.

"Jo shot at it before. It didn't work."

"Jo shot at a projection of an image, Madeline. If it's a thing of flesh and blood, I'll kill it. If it wants to play mind games with me, I'll handle it. It might be able to control other people's mind, but it can't control mine." Ciaran's eyes darkened as he scanned his gun around the room.

CHAPTER 31

Madeline grabbed the water jug on her bedside table and splattered water around the room. In the corner of the room, the water hit the shape of the beast.

"There!" Madeline yelled and pointed.

Ciaran shot continuously at the shape with his silenced gun.

The beast roared. Its shape flashed and glowed and then faded away.

"I told you—if it has flesh, I'll make it bleed."

Then Ciaran dropped the gun and grabbed his head. He ground his teeth and looked at the corner where the beast had stood before. A vein swelled on his forehead, but he stared steadily at the beast.

Madeline knew it couldn't get inside Ciaran's head. It couldn't control him. As he said, in this mind game, he had won.

Madeline dove and grabbed the gun Ciaran had dropped to the floor, but she couldn't see the beast now. She threw the empty jar at the wall. The shattered glass flew everywhere.

Some of the pieces of broken glass hit the shape of the beast. Madeline fired off two shots, hoping they would do some damage.

Another roar.

Ciaran smiled.

It seemed that the beast knew it couldn't get into Ciaran's head. It roared again and slapped at the gun in Madeline's hand. The blow threw Madeline to the wall, and the gun flew away, falling to the floor.

Ciaran grabbed it and, guessing where the beast would be standing after hitting Madeline, he fired at where its head or vulnerable parts might be.

A scream filled the room.

He must have hit it, Madeline thought.

The noise from the room drew the attention of the medical staff. A nurse rushed inside, but as soon as she entered, her eyes rolled up and she charged at Ciaran. Ciaran said nothing. He stepped forward and hit the nurse in the head. She fell to the floor, unconscious.

"I'm sorry," Ciaran said to the nurse and walked over to help Madeline up.

"You know how this works?" Madeline asked as she rushed out of the room with Ciaran.

"Classic hologames." Ciaran smiled. They ran down the hallway heading out of the hospital and toward Ciaran's car.

Ciaran drove the car out of the hospital's parking lot and headed toward the highway.

"Do you think there will be any more surprises from the beast before we get to Mon Ciel?" Ciaran asked.

"I don't know. It's not in the car, thank God. Can Mon Ciel's protective shield stop it?"

"It works against Sciphils. But I don't know what this thing is. The energy coming from it was similar to what came out of Pete Chandler, Sciphil Nine. I still have to work out the properties of its physical presence—or lack thereof."

"Yes, Ciaran?" Tadgh's voice asked on the speakerphone.

"We're on our way. We'll be at Mon Ciel soon. Could you call and make arrangements for George to come to Mon Ciel? We'll need his expertise again. We will need all of his lighting gear."

A truck sped out from nowhere, aimed straight at Ciaran's car. Ciaran spun the steering wheel, and the car spun and hit a tree.

Ciaran reached over. "Madeline, are you okay?"

"Yes." She worked her way out of the tangled airbag.

Tadgh's voice squeaked out from the phone, dropped somewhere in the car.

Ciaran helped Madeline out.

"You're bleeding." Madeline wiped Ciaran's forehead.

"It's nothing. Let's go."

They ran toward Mon Ciel.

From the truck, two men got out. One man's eyes were rolled up. He ran toward Madeline and Ciaran. The second man trailed behind.

"Stop, stop! What are you doing, Sam?"

Then man called Sam kept running toward Madeline and Ciaran. Ciaran pulled out his gun.

"If he keeps coming at us, I'm going to shoot him," Ciaran said to the second man.

The second man dove and tackled Sam. "Come on, man, what are you doing?" The two men wrestled on the ground.

"You'll have to knock him out, I'm afraid," Ciaran advised.

"What?"

"He won't give up until you knock him out," Madeline added.

A shadow rushed up from behind Ciaran and hit him with a gun barrel. Ciaran fell to the ground. A large man lifted him up and pointed a gun at his head.

Sam sat up, looking at his friend, confused about what was going on. They both looked at the large man, who was, at that point, facing Madeline.

"What the hell are you doing, Dave?" Sam said to the large man.

Madeline could see that Ciaran was down to about twenty percent of his strength and had been dazed by the hit. Dave croaked at Madeline.

"Call Richard."

Madeline hesitated.

Dave pressed his gun harder at Ciaran's head. "I want to talk to Richard."

"Yes. Yes. I will. Don't shoot!" Madeline cried out.

Ciaran used whatever strength he had left to grab the gun. He pivoted and threw Dave to the ground. Dave stood up and roared.

"Stop there or I'll shoot," Ciaran warned.

Dave kept charging, his eyes wild. Ciaran shot him in the hip. He fell, screaming in pain. Madeline picked up Ciaran's gun from the ground. They pointed the guns at the other two men.

"Stay right there," Ciaran said.

Ciaran and Madeline ran toward Mon Ciel.

Behind them, a wedge of wind lifted them up and sent them rolling on the ground. When they got up, they saw the beast—a gigantic half-ape and half-wolf creature—coming toward them.

It was Kyle Wolf in his full form.

CHAPTER 32

Ciaran and Madeline shot at Kyle Wolf. The bullets barely scratched him. Kyle squinted his eyes at Mon Ciel.

Ciaran caught his look. "He can't get inside Mon Ciel, Madeline. Can you make a run for it?"

"I'm not going to run inside and leave you here."

Kyle Wolf roared insanely. His eyes sparked red with fury.

Ciaran pushed Madeline behind him. "We are successors of Sciphils. You're from Eudaiz, and you cannot harm us."

Kyle Wolf stopped.

Silence.

Then he roared again and charged at Ciaran.

Ciaran pushed at Madeline and yelled, "Run!" They moved quickly. But not fast enough.

Kyle seemed to totally ignore Madeline. His enormous ape arm reached out and snatched Ciaran as if he were a rag doll. Kyle smashed Ciaran's body to the ground as hard as he could then let out an ear-piercing scream.

All three men from the truck fell on the ground, their liquefied brains leaking from their ears.

Ciaran spat out blood.

As soon as Kyle hurt Ciaran, he shrank into a much smaller creature. Ciaran was an official successor, and he could see the effect it had on Kyle.

Madeline rushed in front of Ciaran. She stared at Kyle, ready to take him on.

From behind Madeline, Ciaran stood up. He saw that Kyle had shrunken and seemed to be weakened. Taking the opportunity, Ciaran rushed at him. Kyle was still very strong. Ciaran could normally take him on, but he couldn't now with only twenty percent of his strength left.

After receiving a few good blows to the head from Ciaran, Kyle kicked Ciaran, sending him rolling away on the ground. "See if Bran can protect you now," Kyle laughed.

Madeline stood in front of Ciaran again. Ciaran hoisted himself up from the ground and tried to pull Madeline back. But he didn't even have enough strength to hold onto her. Madeline knew it was hopeless. If Kyle attacked, she would not stand a chance.

Kyle got closer to Madeline.

Just then, they heard the roar of a car engine. The car accelerated, charging at Kyle.

The hit was brutal. Kyle was split almost in half, and the car was crunched up like a piece of scrap metal. Tadgh and Jo crawled out of the wrecked automobile.

Kyle didn't die. He had somehow put his body back together.

Kyle cast a glance at Jo. Suddenly, his eyes softened. In response, Jo pulled out her gun and fired—without any effect.

"He's the one, isn't he? He's the fucking monster that violated you? Tadgh asked. He didn't wait for an answer. He saw it all in Jo's eyes. He pulled out his gun and shot.

Ciaran knew it was hopeless. They couldn't kill Kyle. The beast now advanced on Tadgh.

"I'm the successor of the king Sciphil. You might want to negotiate with me before you do anything rash," Ciaran said.

Kyle snapped back to reality and turned toward Ciaran and Madeline. Ciaran pushed Madeline backward.

But he had no idea how to get out of this one.

He feared this might be the end of them.

A beam of white and blue holocast slashed down right in front of the beast, preventing it from approaching Madeline and Ciaran. Richard stepped out from the circle of light.

"This is not just a holocast," Ciaran said in a low voice. "He's stepping outside it."

Richard drew his sword and charged at Kyle.

An enormous cylinder of wind, made of blue and white light and filled with the tangled shapes of unrecognizable creatures, spun around Madeline and Ciaran. They were surrounded by a wall of sounds so jarring they made their noses bleed.

The smell of electricity and melted plastic and metal thickened the air.

The fight slowed down. From outside the circle of light, they could see that Richard had the current advantage, but both Kyle and Richard had been severely injured.

Kyle charged at Richard. But instead of blocking him this time, Richard simply opened his arms.

"No! Grandfather!" Madeline cried as Kyle's sword pierced through Richard's body.

Kyle roared with fury as Richard slumped to the ground.

"I substitute my life for my granddaughter's claim of her virtuous soul. She is now more qualified than ever. Eudaizian constitution. Clause 1506. Section two. You killed an undefended Sciphil. Not only you are exiled, you are not to set foot in Eudaiz, and your eudqi can never be reconnected."

An inhuman scream split the air. Kyle turned into a creature in werewolf shape and fled. He disappeared into the darkness.

The wind stopped. On the ground lay Richard. He was no more than a heap of burned flesh and material.

Madeline scrambled toward him. She picked him up and cradled him in her arms. "Grandfather . . ."

Richard smiled. For the first time, Madeline saw his smile as a granddaughter looking at her grandfather.

"I'm sorry I lost you when you were barely a month old. I couldn't protect you. I can't even take you to the gate now. I'm just an old man, you see."

Madeline wept. Her tears fell on his burned flesh.

"Nobody has ever shed tears for me, Madeline. You are a good woman. Your sixth sense is your talent. You are a just person. A better Sciphil than I could ever be. You will serve Eudaiz well."

"Please don't die, Grandfather. You haven't given me any training. I need your guidance."

"I have authorized Ayana to take you through the gate. Give me your hand."

Richard burned a seal on Madeline's right forearm. Then he closed his eyes for a short moment. He was quickly running out of breath.

"Promise me you will be a good Sciphil."

Madeline nodded, her tears raining on Richard's body. Richard glanced toward Ciaran. He had no more strength to call out. But Ciaran understood and came over to crouch beside Madeline. "I trust you will be a just ruler of Eudaiz," said Richard. "Promise me you will keep my granddaughter safe?"

Ciaran nodded.

"Kyle Wolf used to be Sciphil Four. He betrayed Eudaiz for the Black Rock. I knew but had no evidence against him. Bran didn't believe me. Kyle wanted your mother to be his wife—he wanted her innocence. I promised your mother to him only to bide my time. Your mother ran off to marry her true love, your father. When the Black Rock killed your parents, I was too late to save them. When I came back, you were gone. I didn't know Kyle had anything to do with this. Not until yesterday . . ." Richard was fading rapidly. His voice was barely audible.

"Is there anything I can do for you, Richard?" Ciaran asked.

"No, my time is up . . . I don't know how Kyle got here. But I know he wants to come back to Eudaiz . . . He'll need the gate opened. I warned Ayana . . . Kyle is evil, and he's invincible . . . Ciaran . . . Promise me you'll protect my granddaughter . . ."

Richard's voice trailed off, and he drew in his last breath. His body dissolved into ash and vanished into the air.

Ciaran pulled Madeline into his arms where she wept for the grandfather she had never known.

CHAPTER 33

Mon Ciel had returned to its elegant quietness. Tadgh looked at the picture of his family in their happy times—his father and mother holding Ciaran and him in their arms. Ciaran and he were mere toddlers at the time, but Tadgh remembered every moment of it.

He craved that happy time so much. But they hadn't had that since the day his father died.

Ciaran would have to go to another universe to fulfill his duty to whoever was out there. *But does that mean he has to leave everything behind?* Tadgh wondered.

Tadgh shook his head. He didn't want to think about it anymore. He flopped down onto the day bed and stretched out.

Someone knocked on the door.

"It's open." He didn't bother to open his eyes. Lindsay and Doctor Thomas had talked about rearranging some of the facilities and equipment inside Mon Ciel. He could feign ignorance, as he usually did, but perhaps it was time for him to take on some of the family responsibilities.

It was time to grow up.

The room was strange. Quiet.

Maybe he should practice his newfound ability. For his first exercise, he channeled his thoughts at Jo. At her emotions. He could again see her feelings. This time, they were as clear as crystal. Pure and directed in one direction—toward him.

He opened his eyes to find gracious Jo smiling at him.

He hopped up and grabbed her. She jumped up and wrapped her legs around his waist. He rushed over to the bed and then gently lay her down. He just wanted to admire her foxy face and her gorgeous green eyes. He played with the raven black hair that fell to grace her fragile shoulders.

"I lied to you before. I'm a long-term kind of guy."

She smiled. "I can tell. But now that you can read my emotions, I don't have to tell you about my feelings, do I?"

"Thank you."

"For what?"

"For giving me a chance. I know I'm not your type." Tadgh grinned.

"I bet there's a long list of girls waiting for you who *are* your type. Why me?"

"I don't know. I'm not philosophical about this."

Jo smiled and shrieked with pleasure when Tadgh's hands traveled all over her body. Migi the cat pushed the door open. TJ followed submissively, wearing the sweet puppy look he only used when he asked for treats.

"Come on! Can we please have some privacy here? I bet you two don't do that to Ciaran and Madeline," Tadgh grumbled.

Jo pulled Tadgh's face back to her and kissed him. "Let them watch at their own risk."

"But TJ is under age. Now, Migi? Take TJ out," Tadgh directed.

The gigantic cat wagged her twin tails in disagreement, but then grabbed TJ by the crook of his neck and strode out of the room.

Tadgh turned back to Jo, but before he could say anything, she flipped him over so that he was on his back. Together, they flew into a heated passion that helped them forget the world around them.

***

In Ciaran's room, Madeline curled into his arms. She traced her finger over the seal burned into his right arm and the tattoo of the key that looked like a crucifix from her angle. "So what does the whole thing make us, Ciaran? What are we?"

"I hope we're humans. But that's inconclusive at this juncture. It doesn't matter where we were born, it's our action that determines our humanity. I thought I knew who I was . . . what I was. But now I think I need a lot more information to draw any conclusions."

"It seems to me that the Sciphils are humans, judging by the way they recruit people from Earth. But the citizens of Eudaiz seem to be aliens."

"By that, I hope you don't think of them like little green men. What we're dealing with is not just space travel and different planets. We're talking about *dimensional* travel. Different universes.

Different worlds. I can't even tell you how far or how close their proximity is to Earth."

"You're saying space travel is simple?"

Ciaran chuckled. "Not at all. But you and I will be entering a different world, Madeline. Going through the Daimon Gate to Eudaiz might not be as complicated as what we know as space travel on Earth. It might be as simple as crossing a few dimensions. Maybe that world co-exists with this world, right next to us. Right here." He reached out his hand and made a grabbing gesture into the air.

Madeline rolled her eyes. "Well, that seems simple!"

Ciaran kissed the dimple on her left cheek. "Whatever that world is going to be, as long as we're together, that's what matters most to me."

"Humm, so you're going to be the king Sciphil. Will you have a harem?"

"That's desirable, of course. But you will be Sciphil One. I'm not sure about the political system of Eudaiz, but it sounds kind of like you will be the first councillor. So you will get to approve of my harem." He started kissing her lips, and his hands had suddenly become very busy on her body.

"What if we can't pass the Daimon Gate? I didn't receive any training. You did, but not all of it. What if I'm not qualified to be a Sciphil? Will they send me back to Earth? And can we come back to Earth after you and I become Sciphils . . ." she trailed off, moaning in pleasure as his hands attacked all the right spots.

"Can we worry about that tomorrow? At the moment, I just want to focus on my world, right now and right here, with you."

Her body was tensed up like a bow now. "Ayana said it will be only a few days until we have to go through the Daimon Gate . . ."

"Not so fast. The next destination will still be on Earth, with a real physical location—Australia."

Her breathing intensified, and her system was heading toward an explosion of pleasure. "Let's see if I can identify the right spot . . ." Ciaran said and pushed.

"Yes! Yes!" she cried out, her voice slurred with pleasure.

He laughed, and she flipped him over so he lay on his back. "Not so fast, my king. I don't need to be a psychic to find this location." And she took over.

Together, they traveled to an elusive world of pleasure.

This is the end of
Elusive Beings - A Shade of Mind - Book 3

THE FINAL BOOK IN THE SERIES

Imperfect Divine - A Shade of Mind - Book 4

IS AVAILABLE HERE

Narrativeland.com/shade

A SHADE OF MIND
BOOK 4

IMPERFECT DIVINE

PROLOGUE

.-.-.-.

Her high heels clicked on the hard cold cobblestones of the dark alley. The unpleasant sound echoed back and forth between the narrow stone fences along the sides of the road. Fog crept up from the ground and brushed her long legs that the thermal stockings didn't give much warmth to.

She regretted taking this shortcut already.

But at the other end of this alley, a surprise birthday party was waiting for her. Well, not really much of a surprise since she knew about it. Her best friend had tipped her off by asking her to wear something nice for their girls' night out.

She smiled to herself and tried to ignore the eerie ambiance surrounding her. She was turning eighteen.

Soon.

She heard the sound of flapping wings. This area was notorious for bats—one of those animals she didn't care much for. It had to be an enormous bat by the sound of it. She looked up but saw nothing but the dark sky.

She put her head down and kept walking, pulling out her cell phone to call her friends. No signal. "I'm in the middle of the town, for God's sake!" she cursed to no one in particular and picked up her pace.

Her footsteps echoed louder and louder in the dark alley. Or maybe it was just in her head.

But she wasn't hearing her footsteps now. She was hearing someone else's. She turned around, but there was nothing but a long, dark alley. Reaching the other end where she could see a dim light would be faster than going back.

She could see traffic and pedestrians in the distance. Seeing people made her feel a lot better. She kept walking.

Suddenly, the metallic stench of blood engulfed her. It was so overwhelming she had to gasp to draw in air. The shadow of a man stepped out in front of her, from . . . nowhere. He cast a glance at her with his flaming red eyes. And he smirked.

It was a smirk of victory and satisfaction as if he had just found a long lost treasure.

She froze. She wasn't scared. She didn't pass out. She just couldn't move.

Then a cold blast of air invaded her. It felt like ants crawling all over her body. Her mind was numb. Something was clawing at her soul, seeping into every cell of her body, ripping the dignity out of her.

Every thought she had in her mind. All of her secrets. All aspects of her life. Everything was exposed.

All of her memories of her sweet childhood, of her friends, of her family were leaving her. Bit by bit. The pain in her heart was unbearable.

She was fully awake, lying on the cold cobblestones and watching the last drop of her innocence leaving her. She blinked. And then she saw it. In front and on top of her was the perfect picture of evil.

CHAPTER 1

.-.-.-.

The sound of Jo's voice echoing through the intercom sent Ciaran and Madeline charging up the stairs. They stormed into Tadgh's room, finding him lying flat on the floor, unconscious.

Ciaran took Tadgh's pulse. *Steady*, he mused. His brother was clinically alive and well.

But something was missing inside Tadgh. Something profound. Fundamental. Something that, as a scientist, he didn't care to speak of or even theorize.

Tadgh's soul is gone.

Ciaran shook his head. He couldn't believe he'd let that thought cross his mind. He had no idea how to explain this. Fear clawed at him.

He could cure his little brother of any earthly problem that could be scientifically explained. He had even manufactured the perfect level of sugar in Tadgh's blood—a minor issue Tadgh had when he was a kid.

Ciaran could even help with anything physiological or emotional his little brother might encounter. But the only thing he couldn't help Tadgh with was his mind.

That was the most scientific he could make it. Calling it *the mind.*

When it came to something as metaphysical as a soul, Ciaran didn't even know where to begin.

"How could this happen? One minute we were talking, and the next, he fell to the carpet!" Jo exclaimed.

"He's all right, Jo."

"He doesn't look all right, Ciaran. Is he traveling into another dimension like you did the day before yesterday?"

Ciaran shook his head. "Let's put him on the bed."

Madeline nodded. As soon as she grabbed Tadgh's arm to help, she yelped and released it. A tear rolled down her face.

"What is it, Madeline?" Ciaran asked.

Madeline's eyes were glazed for a short moment, and then they became clear again. "He saw Kyle Wolf. But not via his own eyes," she whispered.

"So whose eyes did he see the monster through?" Ciaran muttered, more to himself than to Madeline. It a rhetorical question. He didn't think Madeline knew the answer. But he had a feeling someone did. Ciaran looked at Jo.

The blood drained from Jo's face. "The eyes of the victim. He could see their emotion and the monster's emotion. He saw Kyle's satisfaction when he ripped the innocence out of someone. Like he once did to me," Jo spoke under her breath.

Ciaran grabbed Madeline's cold, shaky hands. "Sit down, will you?" He nudged her down onto a chair.

"It's horrible." A tear rolled down Madeline's face.

"Let it calm down. It will pass." He kissed her lightly. "Okay?" he asked. She nodded.

On the floor, Tadgh stirred, and his eyes fluttered and opened. Ciaran darted over. Tadgh's eyes were distant, as if he hadn't yet come back to reality. Then in a brief second, Ciaran knew his brother was back.

"Tadgh, you passed out. You remember anything?" Ciaran reached his hand out to pull him up.

Tadgh glanced around the room. He paused at Jo's face. Then his eyes hardened. The darkness in his brother's eyes worried Ciaran. "You can see emotion since you stupidly injected the poison into your body, but it shouldn't force you to *connect* with Kyle."

"No way am I connected with that monster. I don't have a choice here. I see what I see," Tadgh muttered. "Fuck this!" Tadgh kicked the chair, the table, and another piece of furniture as he moved across the room. Ciaran let him go for a couple of minutes then tackled him to the floor.

"Let go of me." Tadgh shoved Ciaran off and stood up.

"Do I have to assign security and keep you chained up, Tadgh? We're going to Australia tomorrow . . ."

"I'm going with you," Tadgh snarled.

"Give me a very good reason to allow that, Tadgh."

"I need to kill the fucking bastard."

"What did you see?"

"Can't tell you. And there's nothing you can do."

"You can't be sure of that," Ciaran countered.

Tadgh stared at Ciaran and said nothing more.

"Very well, you will stay here. I'll assign security and take away all of your access to transport." Ciaran strode toward the door of the room.

Tadgh darted after him and grabbed for Ciaran's shoulder. The momentum of Tadgh's hand pushed Ciaran, shoving him forward. "Don't be ridiculous, Ciaran. I can help you."

Entering the reception room at the end of the corridor, Ciaran turned around. "I said no. You and Jo stay here. I can't take care of you in Australia."

"Let me put this another way, big brother. How can you be so sure Kyle wouldn't try to kill *you* in Australia?" Tadgh cocked an eyebrow in challenge. "I need to go with you."

"Then tell me what you just saw."

"Kyle was doing what he did to Jo to another girl in London," Tadgh said and glanced at Jo.

"How did you see it? I could feel the vibration of Kyle's energy when I touched your arm," Madeline said.

Tadgh shook his head. "I didn't see much. Just got a glimpse of objects and shapes, and I heard some sounds. The shapes and sounds translate into emotion. That's what I feel. I extrapolate the action that cause the emotion and the owner of the emotions afterward."

Tadgh flopped into a reading chair and closed his eyes.

"And you did all that in a few minutes?" Jo asked.

"He's a walking, talking computer, Jo," Ciaran said.

"I can tell if Kyle is coming when he's miles away. Like now. He's in London. I can't tell the precise location. But if he takes any action on anyone, I can tell from miles away," Tadgh said.

"I can't risk him controlling you. Madeline and Jo saw that happen," Ciaran explained.

"Madeline knocked me out way before they could even tell if I was able to resist Kyle."

Ciaran looked at Madeline. She nodded to confirm what Tadgh had just said.

Tadgh grunted and held his head.

"I'll have to knock you out, Tadgh," Ciaran said.

Tadgh gestured for Ciaran to stay away. "It wasn't Kyle. It's the girl . . ." he grunted again and looked as if he was in excruciating pain. Ciaran approached.

"No, no. I can take this." Tadgh held his head and closed his eyes. After a while, he opened his eyes and looked at Ciaran. He was as white as a ghost.

"Turn on the news," Tadgh said numbly.

Ciaran turned on their private channel. As the latest news flashed, the blood drained from all of their faces.

CHAPTER 2

.-.-.-.

Kyle smiled to himself. He stood right in front of the small pub where his latest prey was doing whatever he made her do. He frowned. He had to be careful. He needed quite a few more innocent souls before he could crash the Daimon Gate opening in Australia. There was no room for error.

The attempt tonight had been a success, which pleased him a great deal. An eighteen-year-old girl in a dark alley. A weak-willed soul—and to his delight—a virtuous one.

Kyle chuckled and focused his gaze through the pub's small window to enjoy his victory. Nobody could see him unless he allowed them to. He was invisible to the naked eye. Yet the damage he did to the humans was quite visible.

He could stand right inside the pub, and all would be oblivious to his existence. He would probably enjoy the smoky ambiance where the humans congregated and tried to give one another lung cancer. The stench of fresh blood was pleasant to him. And he would certainly like the sound of metal and glass cutting into flesh. His senses had become a lot more acute these days.

But no. He didn't want to mix with humans. He was once a Eudaizian, a citizen of a beautiful universe in which he was born—and which he still longed for. He would forever be a Eudaizian in his heart, even though they had exiled him and stripped him of all his rights.

Well, he would take all of those rights back.

Soon.

Chaos in the pub. Screams. Cries. Crashes. Blood splattered onto the windows. People shoved at the heavy oak door and stormed outside.

The young girl grabbed a knife, possibly a steak knife, and slaughtered everyone in her way. She was especially interested in those that holding balloons and banners for the surprise birthday party.

He had heard that thought screaming in the girl's head when he had raped her soul. After thirty-three years living on this hell hole called Earth, he had learned what birthdays meant to humans. He still couldn't understand why they celebrated their earthly existence when the soul meant so much more than the body.

Kyle shook his head. Anyway, who cared?

He didn't care how many people the girl was killing in the pub. Those casualties didn't count on his score card. The innocent soul of the girl counted, though. She counted as one.

Kyle sighed. He needed more than that. So he needed the girl to hurry up, kill someone, and then kill herself. That was the final tick in the box to ensure that tonight was a success.

Police sirens echoed in the distance. He should help the girl before people talked her out of the final step, the last step in being his score.

Kyle closed his eyes. When he opened them, the girl appeared on the roof of the building. She looked down as if scared. Tears streamed down her face. Her hair flew and tangled in the winter wind. She held onto the chimney.

"Come on, darling. Jump. I'll catch your soul," Kyle mumbled to himself.

The girl started to cry, and her legs began to wobble. She hung on tightly and leaned on the chimney so that her knees wouldn't buckle.

"It's all right. It won't be bad at all. Come on, sweetheart. I'll take you to heaven. Come to me," Kyle whispered.

The girl cried out loud. Kyle knew too well that she was at the extreme of her conflicting emotions. He couldn't let her give in to her survival instinct or his attempt would be ruined. He couldn't let the girl do the opposite of what he wanted her to do.

Kyle Wolf had never been defeated in that way.

He closed his eyes and chanted an ancient spell. This was his last resource. He'd never had to rely on magic before. Ever. Magic was what ruined his Master. But he had no choice now. He cast the spell.

And in no time, the girl's body landed in front of the cameraman of the news crew who had just arrived on the scene.

Kyle smiled. *Success.* He turned around to hunt for a few more souls.

CHAPTER 3

.-.-.-.

Ciaran's little hands gripped the ledge outside his room's window tightly, and he climbed out to the roof. There was no way he was going to be grounded in his room for a week. He was four, and he was entitled to make a case with his father. If Father listened.

Father always encouraged Tadgh to talk. And that was fair enough because his brother was just learning to talk. But Ciaran knew he was able to speak at a level beyond his age. If it wasn't true, would Father have given him books in philosophy last year?

So why had Father just grounded him this time without even listening to his reasons?

Those wild dogs had attacked and killed Dew, his German shepherd. What was wrong with a little retaliation?

And he didn't do much damage or hurt anyone. He had mixed the explosive, and he'd tested it on the statue of the Goddess of Kindness in the garden. It was only a statue! And he didn't blow up the whole thing . . . just the head.

So why was father so upset?

Ciaran looked down the slope of the roof. It was quite steep. But that was all right. He had strong grip.

He scooted his bare little feet along the roof tiles, carefully lowered himself down to the gutter, and then dropped down to the ground. He pulled out the slippers he had folded into the pockets of his pajamas, put them on, and strode toward the back garden.

Soon he stood at the hill at the back of Mon Ciel.

The dark hill was covered with bushes, ancient trees, and numerous paths that led to places in the woods where Father would never let him go. Ciaran wasn't afraid of the dark—or anything else for that matter. He was willing to explore and learn.

What was wrong with Father lately?

He missed Dew. Until his little brother had grown up and could speak a bit more, Dew had been his only friend. He looked up the hill to where the wild dogs had killed his dog, and he ground his teeth.

He hated those dogs.

He knew his father wouldn't approve of such strong emotion. A kid his age wasn't supposed to feel hatred—or even know what it meant.

But he really missed Dew. A tear rolled down his face. And that was what he couldn't allow.

He was four.

He was a big brother.

And he would not cry.

The fury had blasted at him then for the first time. He didn't know where it had come from, but he knew he was furious. His temperature increased. His blood boiled. His head felt as if it was going to explode.

The next thing he knew, blades of something hit the forest in front of him with incredible force. Trees were trimmed down to the roots. Dirt, grass, and rocks flew into the air as the gigantic blades hit the ground, chopping everything in their path.

The blades spun and flew around like gigantic fans from alien spaceships. In seconds, they had carved the hill down to its bare rock bed. He was sure that all the ancient trees and animals in the little forest had been exterminated.

Ciaran fell on his backside. He knew the blades had come from his mind. They were a tangible form of his fury. They came from his thoughts of killing.

In front of him now was the scene of a war zone.

Now he understood why his father had worked so hard to teach him to control his temper. Why his father had tried everything in his power to stop any trace of violence in his thought processes.

His father had to talk him out of violence without being able to give examples or demonstrations of the consequences if he did otherwise. Because *this* was a live demonstration of what could happen. If there had been anyone in the forest during that time, their lives were lost. He hoped there had been no one lurking in the bushes in the middle of this winter night.

But he would never know.

Another tear fell onto his cheek. Now he was upset because he wasn't allowed to be upset anymore. He wondered what would happen if he cried.

For a limited time, D.N. Leo gives away
4 books (e-version) in the Multiverse Collection

CLAIM YOUR BOOKS
http://narrativeland.com

THANK YOU FOR READING!
D.N. LEO

He dare not try. He didn't even want to think about it.

Ciaran went quietly home and climbed back into his room.

"Ciaran!" Madeline called him from behind, snapping him back to reality. He was staring at the very window that he had climbed out on his way to experience the power of his fury for the first time.

He turned around and smiled at her.

"What are you doing here?" she asked.

"This was my room when I was a kid."

"Oh . . ." Madeline looked around. Then she embraced him. It embarrassed him how much he had grown to crave her embraces. He held her in his arms and looked out the window.

When they had seen the news and realized Kyle had possessed the girl in London and had told her to kill herself and the others, Madeline had called Kyle a monster. What would she think if she knew his mind had a destructive power that made Kyle's ability look like child's play? What she would think of him if she knew he could kill—and did kill—with just a thought?

He kissed the dimple of her left cheek, then he looked into her eyes. "I need to tell you something."

A Shade of Mind Series
Www.narrativeland.com/shade

1-4 Random Psychic
2-4 Forever Mortal
3-4 Elusive Beings
4-4 Imperfect Divine

D.N. LEO 'S NOVELS
SERIES READING ORDER

http://www.narrativeland.com/dnleo-series-reading-order

A SHADE OF MIND

(narrativeland.com/shade)

The Journey from Earth to Euдaiz

Main Characters: Ciaran, Madeline, Tadgh, and Jo

(Recommended reading in order)

1-4 Random Psychic

2-4 Forever Mortal

3-4 Elusive Beings

4-4 Imperfect Divine

—

SPECTRUM

(narrativeland.com/spectrum)

Main characters: Lorcan, Orla, Roy and Mori

(Recommended reading in order)

1-4 White Curse

2-4 Blue Fox

3-4 Indigo Stone

4-4 Red Moon

—

MINDSCAPE

(narrativeland.com/mind)

Main characters:

Ciaran, Madeline, Tadgh, Jo, Kyle, Hoyt, Ayana, Pete, Sizx, Lorcan, Orla

(Recommended reading in order within series, can be read in ANY order in related to other series)

1-6 Queen's Gambit
2.- Knight & Pawn
3-6 Lone Castle
4-6 Doubled Bishops
5-6 Dead Squares
6-6 King's Endgame

—

SILVER BLOOD
Main characters:
(narrativeland.com/silver)
Ciaran, Madeline, Tadgh, Jo, Caedmon, Sedna, Roy, Mori, Zach, Mya, Lorcan and Orla
This series can be read in ANY order within the series and in related to other series.

Virgo
Libra
Scorpio
Taurus
Pisces
Gemini

Thank you for reading.

If you enjoyed reading **Elusive Beings**, I would appreciate it if you would help others enjoy this book, too.

<u>Recommend it.</u> Please help other readers find this book by recommending it to friends, readers' groups and discussion boards.

<u>Review it.</u> Please tell other readers why you liked this book by reviewing it. A few sentences will make a significant difference to me. If you do write a review, please send me an email at info@dnleo.com so I can thank you with a personal email.

Connect with me online:
Web: narrativeland.com; Twitter: @dnleostory

To join my mailing list, please click here

Facebook page of the Outlanders of the Multiverse series
https://www.facebook.com/Outlandersofthemultiverse

COPYRIGHT

ELUSIVE BEINGS
A Shade of Mind - Book 3

By D.N. Leo

I greatly appreciate you taking the time to read my work. Please consider leaving a review wherever you purchased the book, and refer the book to your friends.